Perfecting Fiona

Perfecting Fiona

Marion Chesney

St. Martin's Press / New York

Library of Congress Cataloging-in-Publication Data

Chesney, Marion.
    Perfecting Fiona.

    (The School for manners ; 2nd)
    I. Title. II. Series: Chesney, Marion. School for
manners ; 2nd.
PR6053.H4535P47 1989   823'.914   88-30516
ISBN 0-312-02577-7

First Edition
10 9 8 7 6 5 4 3 2 1

For Sue Austin
With love

Perfecting Fiona

Chapter 1

A young unmarried man, with a good name
And fortune, has an awkward part to play;
For good society is but a game,
"The royal game of Goose," as I might say,
Where everybody has some separate aim,
An end to answer, or a plan to lay—
The single ladies wishing to be double,
The married ones to save the virgins trouble.
—Lord Byron

𝒯O PRACTISE ECONOMY WAS to be out of fashion. And so those two professional chaperones, Effy and Amy Tribble, were soon hard pressed.

Both were maiden ladies of a certain age, fallen on hard times. They had, on receiving their last piece of bad news—a dying relative had cut them out of her will—decided to go into business. They were well connected and had a fairly fashionable London address. And so they advertised themselves as chaperones, not to any ordinary misses, but to the difficult ones, the spoilt ones, the seemingly unmarriageable ones.

They had already had one great success, but strangely enough, offers for their services had not come flooding in. The fact was that society members felt that to engage the services of the Tribble sisters was to advertise to the world that one's offspring was, to say the least of it, "difficult."

Their first "job" had paid generously and the Tribbles had enjoyed their first taste of luxury in a long time. But the inflationary prices of the Regency soon began to make enormous inroads in their capital.

And so, on one cold winter's day when London lay under a blanket of suffocating fog, Effy awoke to the sound of whoops of delight from her sister Amy. An offer had arrived in the morning's post.

"Don't be so *noisy*, Amy," wailed Effy, struggling up against her lace-edged pillows as her sister erupted into the bedchamber.

Effy Tribble had gained a delicacy and beauty with age that she had lacked when she was younger. Her fine silver hair curled prettily around a sweet, only slightly wrinkled face. Her hands were still small and white and her tiny feet had high-enough arches to please the most finicky member of society.

Alas for Amy! She had been a plain girl and now was a large, plain, middle-aged woman with a tall flat figure and enormous hands and feet and the face of a trusting horse.

She sat heavily on the end of the bed and crackled open the parchment. "Listen, sis," she cried. "It is from a Mr. and Mrs. Burgess of Tunbridge Wells. They have a niece, Fiona, and they say that despite several advantageous offers, she remains unwed. The gentlemen ask leave to pay their addresses, are left alone with this Fiona, and the next thing the Burgesses know is that the suitor has fled the house, never to be seen again."

Effy sighed. "Oh, if we could only say No. This Fiona sounds a difficult case." Effy could not imagine any lady refusing even one offer.

"Nonsense," said Amy. "I am sure all she needs is a firm hand. How much more difficult our task would seem if the girl was an antidote and not capable of attracting any suitors at all. Let me see, the Burgesses are very hard on her. They say she is bold and brazen. Dear me! Slut on't! We shall come about."

"Do not use foul language, Amy," said Effy primly.

Amy reddened and muttered, "Sorry," and then fell to studying the letter again. "They *do* sound desperate. They will call here on January the fourteenth—that's about a fortnight hence—and if they find us and the accommodation suitable, they will 'deposit' Fiona with us."

"So soon?" wailed Effy.

"Can't be soon enough," said Amy robustly. "Only think! Not so long ago we had very little money and no servants. Now we have a whole houseful of servants to be paid on quarter-day and . . ."

"And no money at all," finished Effy in a hollow voice. "How could we manage to get through so much?"

"Because we are in society," said Amy, "and just being *in* takes a deal of money. Why, even when our last client paid up, we had little compared to others. What of the gentlemen who think nothing of losing thirty thousand pounds of an evening at White's?"

"They are *gentlemen*," said Effy repressively. "It is only the ladies who know how to balance the books and that is why the gentlemen marry us."

"Oh, really?" said Amy cynically. "I thought it was because they wanted a legitimate ride at home instead of playing the beast with two backs around the brothels. Have you ever considered how many of our Pinks of the Ton must be Frenchified?"

"*AMY!*" screeched Effy, clapping her hands over her ears. "Frenchified" was cant for contracting venereal disease.

Amy paid her no heed. "Mr. Haddon calls today. He will be glad to hear our news."

Effy dropped her hands. "Mr. Haddon! Why did you not warn me?"

Mr. Haddon was a nabob, and a friend of the sisters. Effy was always sure Mr. Haddon was on the point of proposing to her—an assumption which never failed to infuriate Amy.

"I must see Mamselle Yvette right away," said Effy, getting out of bed. "She must finish that scarlet merino gown for me directly." Mamselle Yvette was another of the sisters' extravagances—a resident French dressmaker.

"Mr. Haddon is an old friend," said Amy sulkily. "No need to primp and fuss."

"There is always need," said Effy, pulling on a lacy wrapper. She then gently removed a confection of a nightcap to reveal a headful of curl papers. "My efforts have not been in vain in the past. To think I could have been married were it not for . . . Ah, well, no use crying over spilt milk."

Amy flapped her large feet in embarrassment. Effy always claimed that her single state was due to her determination not to desert Amy. But it was Amy who had been nagged out of accepting two respectable proposals by Effy, a fact that Amy, who did not think much of herself, often forgot.

She wrapped her shawl more tightly about her shoulders, for her thin muslin gown was not adequate protection against the winter draughts which whistled under

4

every door of the house in Holles Street. Yvette, the French dressmaker, had tried to persuade Amy to adopt the new military style of dress for ladies, feeling that a more mannish mode of dress would flatter Amy's flat figure. But Amy, after reluctantly agreeing to the making of two gowns, became convinced that if she dressed in a young fashion, then she would *look* young, so her gown was of pink muslin with a low neckline and little puffed sleeves.

She sighed and went off to inspect the household books, and to see if any more extravagances could be pared from the budget.

And yet the expenditure of the Tribble sisters seemed downright parsimonious compared to that of other members of the ton.

The Prince Regent's capacity for spending money was shared by the whole of society. A hostess who was in the grip of one of the latest crazes of interior design and wanted her whole house done over in the Egyptian mode thought nothing of piling all the old furniture—Sheraton, Chippendale, and Wyatt—onto the lawn and making a bonfire of it. To make a brave appearance riding in the Park was far more important to a gentleman than his bank balance, and aristocrats like the humpbacked Lord Sefton cheerfully paid a thousand guineas at Tattersall's for a thoroughbred.

Amy, who enjoyed riding, hired a horse from John Tilbury of Mount Street for twelve guineas a month, and that did not cover the animal's keep.

Clothes were another extravagance. A simple muslin evening gown could end up costing a fortune, for often the clasps on the bodice were made of gold and precious stones and the embroidery was of gold thread and seed pearls. Fine lace was so expensive that each lady's maid had a lace box to guard as well as a jewel box.

5

Amy's head was soon aching after studying the books. Mrs. Lamont, the housekeeper, protested that Amy did not trust her and threw her apron over her head and burst into tears and had to be soothed down with gin and hot water.

Feeling frazzled, Amy decided to go out riding as soon as Mr. Haddon's visit was over. She changed into a smart bottle-green riding dress of mannish cut which became her better than anything else she had in her wardrobe. But Amy did not know that. In her mind, she had given up any hope of attracting Mr. Haddon. Let Effy flutter and flirt and tease. Amy decided she would rise above it all.

She sat down at the toilet table and let Baxter, the lady's maid, arrange her hair. Baxter was a tall, gaunt elderly woman, former lady's maid to the aunt who had failed to leave the Tribbles any money in her will. She was a conscientious woman and felt Amy was a perpetual walking slur on her art.

She picked up Amy's heavy iron-grey tresses. "Have you ever thought of a leetle dye, mum?"

"No, I have not," snapped Amy, who often thought of dying her depressing locks but had not the courage to do so.

"Or one of the new cuts? I would not do it myself, of course," said Baxter, lighting the spirit lamp to heat the curling tongs. "But I could get Monsieur André, who—"

"Enough," said Amy crossly. She was a tall woman, but Baxter always left her feeling diminished in size and spirit. "Monsieur André is too expensive and that you know. Get on with it, Baxter."

Baxter primped her lips in disapproval, and after combing a solution of sugar and water through Amy's hair to stiffen it, began to curl it all over her head.

Yvette, the dressmaker, entered quietly and stood watching the operation.

6

"What are you staring at, Frenchie?" grumbled Baxter.

"I do not think Miss Amy should have the curls," said Yvette. Baxter's bosom swelled with outrage. She was jealous of Yvette, who was young and attractive in a sallow-skinned, black-eyed way. "Don't you dare tell me how to do my job," she said.

Yvette sighed and tried again, appealing to Amy directly. "The curls are not for you, ma'am. Perhaps one of the new Roman styles with the hair swept back from the forehead and perhaps ringlets falling from the crown, but not curls."

"Leave me alone, both of you," cried Amy, starting up so suddenly that the curling tongs went flying.

She marched down to the drawing room, a high colour on her cheeks, to find that Mr. Haddon was already there and being entertained by Effy, who was wearing her new gown of scarlet merino. Looks like a tart, thought Amy viciously.

Mr. Haddon rose courteously at Amy's entrance. He was a tall, thin, slightly stooped man with pepper-and-salt hair tied back at the nape of his neck with a ribbon. He had gone out to India a relatively poor young man and had come back a rich nabob. He bowed over Amy's hand, and when she was seated, went back to his own chair beside the tea-tray.

"So," said Effy, "you can see we are all of a dither. I am afraid our new task must be this Fiona, although I had thought, after our last success, that we would have been able to take our pick."

"It takes time to build up a reputation," said Mr. Haddon. "Does this young lady have a good dowry?"

"She is an heiress," said Amy gruffly.

Effy raised plucked eyebrows. "You did not tell me that, Amy."

Amy gave a gauche shrug and stared at the fire as if it were the most interesting fire she had ever seen.

"Then you should have no difficulty," said Mr. Haddon. "It is a sadly materialistic world. Everyone talks of love, but no one marries for it."

"Our last charge did," said Effy.

"Ah, well, there is always the exception to prove the rule."

Effy batted her lamp-blackened eyelashes at Mr. Haddon over the edge of her fan. "Would *you* marry for money, Mr. Haddon?"

"I am a confirmed bachelor, but were I not, then I would not marry for money."

There was a little silence. Amy looked sideways and caught a glimpse of her own reflection in a long looking-glass. An angry middle-aged woman with a ridiculously girlish head of curls stared back.

I have just passed my half century, thought Amy bitterly. "I look it. Effy and I have been dreaming of marriage for so long that we have not noticed the passing of the years. A lot of our contemporaries are dead. We should be studying the latest patterns in shrouds instead of the latest fashions in gowns." Her eyes glittered with tears.

"I see you are dressed for riding, Miss Amy," said Mr. Haddon gently.

"Yes," said Amy hoarsely. She cleared her throat. "Yes," she said again. "My horse is being brought round from Tilbury's."

"And I have *my* mount," said Mr. Haddon, "so we may ride together."

Amy's sudden surge of elation was short-lived. Effy got to her feet and rang the bell. "Then I shall come too," she cried gaily. When the footman answered, she told him to run to Tilbury's and find her a horse.

"But you don't ride!" cried Amy furiously. "You hate it. You said so."

"La, sis, what nonsense you do talk. I quite dote on it."

While Effy went off to change into a riding dress, Mr. Haddon tried to engage Amy in conversation. But the miserable Amy only answered him in gruff monosyllables.

Effy at last appeared in a dainty blue velvet riding dress trimmed with silver.

She chattered on gaily as they left, hanging on to Mr. Haddon's arm as Amy slouched behind them. "I am a veritable Diana, Mr. Haddon," trilled Effy. She stopped short on the doorstep, her mouth fell open and her cheeks blanched. "Such very *tall* horses," she murmured.

Amy's spirits rallied. She felt Effy deserved to be punished. It was balm to her soul to see how terrified Effy was as they rode along Oxford Street. But when they reached the Park and Amy wanted to gallop, Effy screamed that she could not be left alone, and so the horses moved slowly on at an amble.

"You must think me a sad case, Mr. Haddon," cooed Effy. "Now Amy is not afraid. She is quite an Amazon, and does not suffer from any frailties of our gentler sex."

Amy let her horse fall behind Effy's. "Only look over there, Mr. Haddon," cried Amy. "One of the deer has escaped from the enclosure."

As Mr. Haddon looked away, Amy leaned forward and struck Effy's mount across the rump with her whip. Effy's horse went off like the wind, with Effy hanging on for dear life and screaming like a banshee. Mr. Haddon rode in pursuit and Amy rode as well, determined to get to her sister before Mr. Haddon could effect any sort of romantic rescue. But Mr. Haddon had the better horse. He caught up with Effy and seized her horse's reins and brought it to a halt. Effy was sobbing with fright as Mr. Haddon dismounted and lifted her down from the saddle.

"Now, Miss Effy," said Mr. Haddon soothingly. "You are perfectly safe. I do not know what caused that ridiculous animal to bolt like that."

Effy buried her sobbing face in his coat.

Amy sat on her horse and surveyed the scene. Instead of humiliating Effy as she had planned to do, she had succeeded in turning her twin into a maiden in distress. She felt old and gawky and tired. Amy decided there and then to behave herself in future. She had never had any chance of attracting Mr. Benjamin Haddon, and it was folly to think otherwise.

She dismounted and helped Mr. Haddon to soothe Effy. It was a long time before they could persuade Effy to remount and then, riding one on either side, they escorted her back to Holles Street.

Effy promptly retired to her bedchamber. Mr. Haddon stayed to talk to Amy, relieved that his old friend had become easy to chat to again. He did not know that Amy had given up any hope of attracting him for the simple reason he did not for a minute suspect she had ever harboured such hopes. He was only glad that his old friend appeared once more herself and it was with great reluctance that he finally took his leave.

Amy avoided Effy for the rest of the day, hoping to put off the dreaded moment. But it came at last when Effy appeared at the dinner table. "Did you see how he held me to his bosom, Amy?" cried Effy as soon as they were both seated.

"Turtle soup," said Amy, putting down her spoon. "I really must speak sternly to Mrs. Lamont. We cannot afford turtle soup."

"And the speaking look in his eye," said Effy dreamily. "It was the most romantical thing imaginable. I thought my last moment had come. I could see the trees hurtling past. I could feel myself slipping from the saddle to be pounded under the horse's hooves. And then *he* was there, holding me in his strong arms . . ."

"Drink your soup, in the name of a whore's bum," shouted Amy suddenly. "It cost a fortune!"

"So remember at all times that the Tribble sisters are *ladies!*" said Mrs. Burgess two weeks later as their carriage entered the outskirts of London.

"Of course, Aunt," said Fiona Macleod.

"And if they find you a suitable gentleman, you are to become engaged to him and not cause myself or Mr. Burgess any more trouble."

"Yes, Aunt."

Mrs. Burgess looked suspiciously at her niece, but Fiona's face was hidden by the brim of her bonnet.

Mrs. Burgess had not met either of the Tribble sisters. But Lady Baronsheath's wild daughter had fared well at their hands, and Lady Baronsheath had told Mrs. Toddy who lived in Tunbridge Wells, and Mrs. Toddy had told Lady Fremley, and Lady Fremley had told Mrs. Burgess, which was just about the same as Lady Baronsheath confiding in Mrs. Burgess direct. The Tribble sisters must be ladies of high rank and impeccable manners or Lady Baronsheath would not have engaged their services in the first place.

Perhaps the Tribbles might find out what it was about Fiona that brought suitors up to the mark, only to have them fleeing the house after they had spoken to her. Perhaps it was the Scottish in her, thought Mrs. Burgess disapprovingly. She no longer considered herself Scottish, having married at a young age and moved to England. Fiona was her late sister's daughter. Fiona had been brought up in Aberdeen, a savage and remote place. Lord Byron hailed from there and he had no morals to speak of. It must be something to do with the climate. Mrs. Burgess herself came from Ayrshire. Her sister Alice had married George Macleod, who was in trade, and had moved north to Aberdeen, while Mrs. Burgess had married a gentleman of leisure and had gone south to Tunbridge Wells. But it was the Macleods who had made a fortune out of their jute manufactories in Aberdeen. Both had died of influenza, leaving Fiona, then fourteen and a wealthy heiress, in the care of the Burgesses. She was now nineteen and should have been married and off the Burgesses' hands two years ago, which was when she had received her first proposal of marriage. Mr. and Mrs. Burgess were strict and staid and dull, but they were not mercenary. They were allowed to draw as much money as they wished from Fiona's lawyers until her marriage, but they felt uneasy with the girl in their quiet, dull establishment. They never knew what she was thinking, but they sensed wickedness and slyness in her. All their rages and rows did not seem to ruffle her in the slightest. She was brazen.

Mrs. Burgess's gloomy thoughts were interrupted by the sound of rapidly approaching hooves. Despite the noise made by their carriage rattling over the cobbles, she could hear the fast-approaching thunder, punctuated by wild cries and halloos.

Mr. Burgess, who had been asleep, woke up with a cry of alarm as two light curricles, each with a team of four horses, dashed past their travelling coach, one on either side, leaving only an inch to spare. The Burgesses' horses reared and plunged, the carriage swayed dangerously and then came to a halt. Mrs. Burgess let out a faint scream.

Mr. Burgess opened the trap in the roof with his stick

and called angrily to the coachman. "Are you all right, John? These young hooligans should be horsewhipped."

"Everything right and tight, sir. They've stopped along the road. One o' them's turned and is coming back this way. Probably to see you're all right."

"Then drive on, Jack," said Mrs. Burgess shrilly. "We do not speak to such riff-raff."

"Can't do that, ma'am. He's swung 'is carriage across the front."

"Fiona!" screamed Mrs. Burgess. "What do you think you are doing?" For Fiona had suddenly jerked down the glass with the strap and was leaning out the window. She sank gracefully back in her seat as a tall man appeared.

Mrs. Burgess shuddered. Here was a rake! He had a thin, handsome, dissipated face and very bright blue eyes. He removed his curly brimmed beaver, revealing a head of thick, glossy black hair artistically curled, and made a low bow.

"My apologies," he drawled. "A stupid race, and I would not have frightened you for the world. Allow me to present myself. Lord Peter Havard."

The Burgesses were not melted by the sound of a title. They were gentry and proud of it. They disapproved of the aristocracy when they thought of them, which was seldom. Lady Fremley was bearable only because she was an inhabitant of Tunbridge Wells, and anyone hailing from that sedate spa had an automatic passport to respectability in the Burgesses' eyes.

"I am Miss Fiona Macleod," said that young lady, "and this is my aunt and my uncle, Mr. and Mrs. Burgess from Tunbridge Wells."

Shocked to the core, Mrs. Burgess found her voice. "If you do not wish to distress us further," she said icily, "remove your carriage and let us go on our way."

"Did you win?" asked Fiona. "The race, I mean."

"Yes, Miss Macleod. By a few inches."

"Why not more?"

"Fiona, I shall *slap* you," said Mrs. Burgess between her teeth.

"Because"—Lord Peter smiled ruefully—"I nearly met my match."

Mr. Burgess leaned forward and jerked up the glass. Lord Peter bowed again and disappeared.

"Have you run mad, Fiona?" demanded Mrs. Burgess. "Encouraging the attentions of a rake?"

"Is he a rake?" asked Fiona, her voice full of rare interest. "How can you tell?"

"That is quite enough of that. Oh, we are moving at last. Not another word, Fiona. Pray God these Tribble women are suitable!"

The journey continued in silence. When the carriage finally turned off Oxford Street into Holles Street, Mr. Burgess addressed his wife. "I feel, my dear, that we should . . . er . . . leave Fiona in the carriage while we prepare these good ladies."

"Yes, certainly," said Mrs. Burgess. "It is important that we speak to them in private."

Fiona watched her aunt and uncle mount the steps of a prosperous-looking town house. Then she opened her reticule and took out a book and began to read.

"And so," said Mrs. Burgess half an hour later, "we have warned you about Fiona. She is to marry someone of her own station in life, that is, a member of the gentry. We are not against the army or the navy, are we, Mr. Burgess?"

"No, my dear."

"Or even the clergy or the merchant class. We do not ask that she marries money, she has enough of her own. But she must not encourage adventurers."

Amy spoke up. "And you do not know how it was that your niece managed to frighten off her suitors?"

"No, she simply insisted they had changed their minds. Mr. Burgess himself beat her, but she remained stubborn. She is bold and wicked. I have paid you a large sum in advance, and you may demand more if necessary, for you have a great task in front of you. A rake by the name of Lord Peter Havard was bold enough to address Fiona on the road here. She is to have nothing to do with such a type."

"Lord Peter is the younger son of the Duke of Penshire," said Effy. "Very rich and considered quite a catch."

"Then let someone else catch him," said Mrs. Burgess. "Such a match would be counted as a failure."

Effy looked pleadingly at Amy. Amy knew what that look meant. It meant, do not take this job. But Amy had a parcel of pound notes on her lap, the Burgesses having decided to pay their advance in hard cash, and she could feel the warmth from all that money seeping through her bones.

"Perhaps we should meet our new charge?" she said.

Mrs. Burgess nodded and a footman went to fetch Fiona from the carriage.

Effy and Amy waited for this bold and brazen hussy to burst into the room. She would probably be rebellious, angry, and defiant.

The double doors were opened and a slight figure walked in. Effy and Amy both looked beyond the girl, looking for someone else, but Mrs. Burgess said, "This is my niece, Miss Fiona Macleod. Fiona, make your curtsy to Miss Effy and Miss Amy Tribble."

Amy and Effy stared as if they could not believe their eyes. Fiona Macleod was a waif, albeit a fashionably dressed one. She had a small pale face and large, large eyes that appeared colourless.

15

"Remove your bonnet, Fiona," ordered Mrs. Burgess. Fiona untied the ribbons of her bonnet and took it off. Her hair was thick and fine and slate-coloured. Wispy curly fine tendrils rioted about her pale face.

Those large eyes of hers gazed at the sisters. They held no expression whatsoever.

Poor thing! was Effy's first thought. They have bullied that poor child into a shadow.

Needs feeding and a bit of rouge, thought Amy.

Mrs. Burgess rose to her feet and her husband followed suit. "We shall leave Fiona in your capable hands," she said. "Use the birch if necessary."

"I do not think we shall find that form of discipline necessary," said Amy firmly. "Do you journey back to Tunbridge Wells this evening?"

"No, no." Mrs. Burgess shuddered. "Such a long way. We shall put up at Grillon's Hotel and leave tomorrow."

"Then you may call on Fiona before you leave," said Amy.

"You are being paid to take care of the girl," said Mrs. Burgess coldly. "We shall call again when the engagement is to be announced."

Amy and Effy went downstairs with the Burgesses and saw them out. When they returned, Fiona was sitting by the fire, warming her hands.

"You may retire to your room, child," said Effy. "Our housekeeper, Mrs. Lamont, will show you the way. You must be exhausted after your journey."

"Not at all, ma'am," said Fiona.

"Are you hungry?" asked Amy. "We sit down to dinner in half an hour."

"Oh, yes, ma'am. I am very hungry."

Probably starved the child, thought Amy furiously. Aloud, she said, "Then go to your room and change and you may join us."

Fiona appeared promptly at the dining table exactly half an hour later. Amy was a good judge of fashion for anyone but herself. She noticed Fiona's silk gown was fussy and unbecoming.

Soup was served. Amy took a mouthful and spluttered and then shouted at the new butler, Harris, who was standing at attention. "What is this, cat's urine?"

"It is vegetable soup, ma'am," said the butler in injured tones. "If you will remember, ma'am, you complained that turtle soup was too expensive."

"A pox on the expense and bad cess to the cook," howled Amy. "Make sure the other courses are fit for human consumption."

"Amy!" Effy threw her sister an anguished look.

Amy turned beet-red. "Sorry," she mumbled. "Forgot meself."

Fiona raised her napkin to her lips. Laughter shone in her large eyes, but both sisters had their heads bent over their plates and did not see it.

Chapter 2

Woman, though so kind she seems, will take
your heart and tantalize it,
Were it made of Portland stone, she'd manage
to McAdamize it.

—*James Planche*

IT BECAME CLEAR AFTER only a few weeks of her stay that Fiona Macleod was going to save the Tribble sisters a certain amount of money. The dancing master, the water-colourist, and the Italian tutor were soon cancelled. Fiona did not need any of them.

She danced like an angel, painted highly competent water-colours, and spoke Italian fluently. She had perfect manners and a graceful bearing. Apart from the fact that she was very quiet and shy and withdrawn, there seemed to be no fault in the girl.

Both Effy and Amy decided Mr. and Mrs. Burgess were hard and unnatural people. Still, despite the fact that

19

Fiona was an heiress, they did expect some difficulty in finding her a husband. *They* found her charming and attractive, but *they* were not men. Men, said Effy, were incalculable creatures, given to falling passionately in love with bold misses with pushing ways.

Yet they held back from starting instruction in the important arts of flirting and conversation. Both decided that Fiona was much in need of a period of kindness and rest.

Neither would admit to the other that they found living with Fiona a bit of a strain. She was so very quiet, so very good. Amy felt clumsy and gauche and loud. Effy, who often enjoyed comparing her own delicate appearance favourably with that of her mannish sister, now felt every bit as large and loud and clumsy as Amy.

Had their charge proved as difficult as they had expected, then they would have kept her at home with her schooling and not presented her anywhere until the beginning of the Season. But, although neither would admit it, both longed to be shot of the waif.

And so when an invitation to a ball at the Duke and Duchess of Penshire's town house arrived, they decided to accept. Amy thought guiltily about the ducal son, Lord Peter, and then came to the rapid conclusion that he was no threat. How could such a well-known rake and heartbreaker ever even look at such a one as Fiona.

Effy, too, was anxious to go. Life had become strangely flat and dull now that the spectre of financial ruin had retreated. They were comfortable, and nothing threatened them.

Perhaps it might have added spice to the sisters' life to know that someone was plotting their downfall at that very moment and spent a great deal of time watching the comings and goings at the house in Holles Street.

The villain was Mr. Desmond Callaghan. He was an Exquisite, a Pink of the Ton, a Fribble, who had assiduously cultivated the sisters' aunt, Mrs. Cutworth, to such good effect that the aunt had died leaving the sisters not one penny, but everything to Mr. Callaghan. The sisters, because of this disappointment, had "gone into business" as chaperones. The wealth they had gained through their first job had prompted the furious Mr. Callaghan to believe that the sisters had inveigled all their aunt's money and jewels out of her before her death. In short, they had tricked him, and must be punished. For he, who had expected to gain riches, after many weary hours and days of dancing attendance on the old frump, had found her bequest contained nothing but debts, which the sale of her house only just covered.

He had recently learned of their role as chaperones extraordinary and was now watching and waiting like a cat at a mouse hole for a chance to harm them in some way. He did not for a minute believe they had achieved their new and comfortable style of living through work alone.

He was one of those doubtful young men who managed to get invitations to some of the best houses, but the Duke and Duchess of Penshire were too high up and too rigid to issue an invitation to their ball to such as himself.

The Tribbles' second footman, Frank, was a callow young man with a taste for low taverns into which he often dropped when he was supposed to be delivering cards. Mr. Callaghan followed him into one of these low hostelries and loosened his tongue with drink and therefore found out the movements of the Tribbles.

He knew he could not hope to attend this ball, but he did learn from Frank that the Tribbles' charge was a Miss Macleod, reputed to have enormous wealth.

Mr. Desmond Callaghan decided to find a way of courting Miss Macleod, marrying her, getting her wealth, and spiting the Tribbles at the same time.

It was such a splendid plan that, for the moment, he was content to warm his hands at the fantasy rather than do anything about it.

Amy and Effy were proud of their dressmaker's skill and had left Fiona in Yvette's hands, confident that any ballgown she made would do the girl justice.

But when Fiona appeared before them, ready to go to the ball, they wondered if Yvette had made a dreadful mistake. Fiona looked . . . well . . . *odd*.

They had expected Fiona to wear white muslin. But for some reason, Yvette had chosen to attire Fiona in a slate-blue silk slip with an overdress of pale-green gauze edged with gold. Her hair had been cut short and curled all over her head, that fine, wispy fly-away hair through which the lamplight shone, creating an aureole around Fiona's small head. Had Fiona been posing for an illustration for a fairy-story book, then, thought Amy, she would have been perfectly suitable. But Amy doubted if someone looking like the Queen of the Elves would cause one heart to beat faster at the ball. Gentlemen liked substantial English beauties, tall and well rounded, with plump bosoms and generous hips.

She wanted to tell Fiona to go and put something else on, but the more she thought about it, the more she decided that white muslin, say, would simply make the girl look washed out.

Effy had misgivings but was too taken up with the charms of her own appearance to worry overmuch about Fiona. In any case the girl had money, and money sang a sweeter song to the ears of London society than any siren could conjure up.

Neither thought to tell Fiona how she ought to behave

at the ball. Both were sure she would behave perfectly—
as usual.

Soon they were all standing in the splendour of the
Penshire town house. Other aristocrats might content
themselves with being crammed into one of those tall thin
town houses while in London. The Penshires in Town
maintained the same grandeur as they did in their palace
in the country. Amy, Effy, and Fiona walked through a
chain of rooms with porphyry columns, glittering
chandeliers, and velvet carpets from a side entrance
before reaching the main staircase which soared up to the
ballroom. The duke and duchess had closed the main
front doors and opened up the side door for the guests'
arrival so that everyone could view the downstairs rooms
before ascending to the ballroom. The duke and duchess
were as proud of their great wealth and possessions as if
they had just recently jumped up into the higher ranks of
society from obscurity instead of having been there all
their lives.

Neither of the Tribbles had been inside the Penshires'
town house before, and yet they were not surprised at
receiving an invitation. Even in the all-too-recent days of
their poverty, they had been invited to the best houses.
The Tribbles were bon ton.

As they reached the head of the staircase, Fiona made
her curtsy to the duke and duchess. "Delightful," murmured the duchess, a smile cracking her austere features.

Amy glanced down at Fiona in surprise, but the girl was
moving away into the ballroom and so she could only see
the back of her head.

Effy found three seats for them. "Do not worry, dear,"
she said, pressing Fiona's hand as the first country dance
was announced, "if you are a wallflower at your first
ball."

And then Effy looked up and found five gentlemen

jostling and bowing in front of Fiona and soliciting her to dance.

"Gracious!" said Amy as Fiona selected one of them and walked off onto the floor. "Society must be more money-mad than I had imagined."

"But we didn't tell anyone Fiona was an heiress," said Effy. "And only look at her. She's . . . she's changed somehow. Her eyes are green. Did you know her eyes were green?"

"I think they pick up the colour from what she's wearing," said Amy. "She's certainly more . . . animated."

But animated was too pedestrian a word to describe the change in Fiona. It was as if the girl had been lit up from inside. Her enormous eyes flashed like emeralds, her skin had a healthy tinge of pink, and there was something about her that made everyone look at her.

"Who is she dancing with?" asked Amy. "He is divinely handsome, and just look at those legs!"

"I will find out," said Effy. She looked along the row of chaperones and then went to sit beside one of society's gossips. After a time, she came back and rejoined her sister.

"Captain Freddy Beaumont," said Effy triumphantly. "Bachelor, rich, handsome, rumoured to be planning to sell out, find a wife, and settle down. Could not be better."

Amy raised her quizzing-glass and studied the captain. His nose was perhaps too undistinguished and short, but his chin was firm, his eyes black and sparkling, and his long legs were a delight.

She studied the other guests. "There is a fascinating-looking man over by that pillar under the musicians' gallery," she said. "He is watching Fiona. Find out who he is."

24

Effy went off and returned a few moments later. "That is none other than Lord Peter Havard. Very dangerous."

Amy experienced a qualm of unease. "Do you think, Effy, that Lord Peter got his parents to send those invitations? He is quite a predatory-looking man, you know, and having met Fiona on the road to London, he may have decided to hunt her for sport."

"I should not think so. I had the gossip about him from Mrs. Barnbury, and she said he breaks hearts—but only those of matrons who know very well what they are about. He has never shown any interest in a young miss before."

"I do not like heart-breakers," said Amy roundly. "They usually don't like women one little bit. They like power and they like to be puffed up with vanity."

"But the gentlemen don't really *like* us ladies at all," said Effy. "I mean, they write sonnets and send flowers, but once the novelty has worn off, they prefer their clubs and taverns."

"Mr. Haddon likes us as friends," pointed out Amy.

Effy tittered and waved her fan. "Dear sis. How blind you are! I believe Mr. Haddon to be romantically inclined."

Amy felt a sudden spasm of hate for her sister.

"Heigh-ho! Lud! Lud! We are to be admired, Effy," said Amy. "Both of us nigh in our graves and the one still believing herself an object of attraction."

Effy's face turned a muddy colour under her blanc. She gasped as if she had been struck and tears spurted from her eyes and fell on the satin of her gown. "How cruel," she said. "How monstrous. You are jealous. You have always been jealous . . . you with your red hands and great flat feet."

"A pox on you," grated Amy. "Well, my great flat feet,

25

as you call them, are quite useful." She aimed a massive kick at the spindly leg of the rout chair on which Effy was sitting. The leg splintered and cracked. The chair toppled and Effy with it. Amy, who had forgotten she was wearing her new bronze kid Roman sandals, hopped around the floor, clutching her injured foot and roaring with pain.

Fiona came hurrying towards them, with the captain following behind. "My dear duennas," she cried. "What ails you?"

The very sound of her voice acted on the sisters like magic. Fiona was work and work meant money and money meant comfort for their old age. Work meant Showing a Good Example.

Effy's tears stopped as if a tap behind her eyes had been turned off, Amy stopped hopping and yowling and helped her sister to her feet. "An accident," said Amy. "These chairs are so frail and dear Effy *has* been gaining a teensy bit of weight."

The Duchess of Penshire sailed forward to voice concern and calmly accepted Amy's explanation, although she had seen Amy kick the leg of the chair after quarrelling openly with her sister. The Tribbles were bon ton and Originals and must be indulged. Had a young miss behaved in such a way, it would have caused a scandal.

By the time the Tribbles were reseated, the country dance had finished and a waltz was being announced. Fiona found Lord Peter at her elbow. He smiled and asked her to dance. Fiona mutely showed him her dance card, which was full. He raised his quizzing-glass and studied it, then bowed and moved away.

But he had noted in his mind that Fiona's partner for the supper dance was a Mr. Giles Manfred. He glanced idly around the ballroom and then made his way through to the card-room. Mr. Manfred was standing watching the play.

"Not playing?" asked Lord Peter.

"Egad, Havard. How you startled me," said Mr. Manfred. "No, I lost a packet at White's last night and I am deep in the River Tick. Like a game, but haven't the readies."

"There are other things to play for," drawled Lord Peter.

"House? Estates? Mortgaged to the hilt, dear boy."

"You do have something of value I covet."

"Eh? What?" Mr. Manfred popped his quizzing-glass in his mouth, sucked furiously, took it out and polished it on the sleeve of his jacket and then stared at Lord Peter with one huge magnified eye.

"The supper dance . . . with Miss Macleod."

Mr. Harvard's eyes gleamed. "Piquet or dice?"

"Dice."

"Done!"

Frank, the second footman in the Tribble household, was preparing to go out. It was an important evening. He had gained free time by lying to the butler about his ailing mother. The butler did not know that the second footman's mother had been dead for five years. Frank was to meet Mr. Desmond Callaghan, Gentleman, at the Coal Hole in the Strand. He, a second footman, was going roistering with a gentleman. The first footman was on duty and so he had the tiny bedroom to himself.

He put a small, smoke-blackened tea-kettle on the minuscule fire to boil up water for shaving. When the water was ready, he poured some into a cracked teacup kept for the purpose and drew his solitary well-worn razor several times over the heel of his hand to smooth its edge, dipped his brush worn nearly to the stump in the hot water and passed it gingerly across as much of his face as he intended to shave. When he had finished shaving, he took out of his trunk an old dirty pomatum pot. A modicum of the contents he stroked onto his eyebrows with the tips of two forefingers and then, spreading some more on the palms of his hands, he rubbed it vigorously into his coarse sandy hair. After combing his hair into various different positions and finally settling on the one he judged the most attractive, he dipped the end of a towel into the little shaving water that was left and, twisting it round his right forefinger, passed it gently over his face, avoiding his eyebrows.

Then he drew out from his trunk a calico shirt with linen wristbands and collar which had been worn only twice since its last wash, taking care not to rumple the very showy ruffles at the front. Once the shirt was on, he stuck in three studs connected together with a little gilt chain. Then he insinuated his legs into a pair of white Inexpressibles, fastened the straps at his feet, and strapped up his braces so tightly that he gave the impression of a man being hoisted on high by his trousers. Then he put on a pair of Hessian boots but did not bother to put any stockings on first. Stockings did not show. He attached a pair of tin spurs to his boots in the hope the admiring populace of London might think he had just dismounted, despite the fact that gentlemen did not wear Hessian boots for riding, or indeed affix spurs to them.

Then he put on a queer kind of underwaistcoat which in fact was only a roll collar of rather faded pea-green silk and designed to set off a fine flowered damson silk waistcoat. After buckling on his stock, he put on his best blue coat with the brass buttons. He picked up a pair of sky-blue kid gloves and looked gloomily at the stains on them and then scrubbed at the offending marks with stale breadcrumbs to try to remove them. His Sunday hat, carefully covered with silver paper, was next gently removed from its box and placed on his head, tilted a little to one side to look devil-may-care, but not rakish.

Lastly, he took down a thin black cane with a gilt head and full brown tassel from a peg behind the door. He surveyed himself in an old greenish looking-glass that was propped up in a corner of the room.

He was not so very bad-looking, despite his coarse sandy hair. His forehead *was* a bit narrow and his eyes were slightly protruberant, but his mouth was well-shaped and firm, always hanging slightly open to show good teeth.

Soon Frank was setting forth down Holles Street and turning the corner into Oxford Street. A street urchin shouted, "My eyes. A'n't that a swell!" and Frank's chest puffed out and his heart felt fit to burst with the glory of it all.

The Coal Hole, as usual, was full of heat and noise and smoke. There was a tiny stage at the end of the taproom on which a buxom girl was dancing with a hoop. Her ankles were bad, noted Frank, drooping his eyelids in what he hoped was a jaded, man-of-the-world way.

Mr. Desmond Callaghan was seated in one of the darkest corners, a fact Frank did not like. He would have liked to be seen drinking with his grand friend at one of the tables in the centre of the room.

The Fribble was wearing a black coat with enormous padded shoulders and a nipped-in waist. His trousers looked as if they had been painted onto his legs and he wore a gold-and-black-striped waistcoat—*very* waspy, as Frank thought with a pang of pure envy.

Mr. Callaghan's first words of greeting to the footman nearly destroyed the new friendship. "Hullo, sailor," he cried. "When did your ship dock?"

Frank half-turned to walk away, so great was his mortification. His blue coat and white trousers had been insulted.

"Sit down, my friend!" added Mr. Callaghan quickly. "You must not mind my jest. I' Faith, I feel outshone."

The ice melted in Frank's vain heart, and he sat down next to Mr. Callaghan.

"Get away without any trouble?" pursued Mr. Callaghan.

"Dev'lish hard," said Frank, attempting a drawl. "But I lied my way to freedom."

All at once, Mr. Callaghan thought he saw a splendid way to make mischief in the Tribble household until such time as he could woo Miss Macleod. He leaned confidentially forward. "It seems a shame that a fine fellow like you should have to work as a servant. . . ." And while Frank, his mouth even more agape than usual, listened avidly, Mr. Callaghan preached the Rights of Man, the Freedom of the Individual in general, and Revolution for the Masses in particular.

Fiona tripped daintily into the supper-room on the arm of Lord Peter Havard. Ladies who had previously that evening thought Miss Macleod a charming creature decided they had been sadly mistaken. She was a wispy, undistinguished thing with bold manners.

Seemingly unaffected by all this burning jealousy, or by the fact that her chaperones were all but standing on their chairs at the far end of the supper-room to make sure Lord Peter was behaving himself, Fiona was answering her partner's questions.

Yes, it was her first Season; no, she did not know London well; yes, she was enjoying herself. Lord Peter did not quite know what to make of her. He had made it his business to find out where Miss Fiona Macleod was residing in London, not a difficult task, as society had quickly made it their business to find out the identity of the Tribble sisters' new charge. That brief meeting on the road had sparked his interest. Learning that Fiona was being brought out by the Tribbles nearly extinguished it, for everyone knew the Tribbles only dealt with "difficult" cases. But what was wrong with Fiona? Her manners were graceful and she danced like an angel.

"I wonder, Miss Macleod," ventured Lord Peter, "why your parents, or perhaps, your aunt and uncle, found it necessary to put you in the care of the Misses Tribble?"

"Why, my lord?" asked Fiona.

"It is rumoured they advertise for 'difficult' misses. Pray, is there anything scandalous about you that I should know, Miss Macleod?"

Fiona wrinkled her brow. "My parents are both dead," she said. "Perhaps I am considered a difficult case because I smell of the shop."

"Indeed!"

"Oh, yes," said Fiona blithely. "My father was in trade. Jute mills."

Lord Peter cynically examined his own slight feeling of shock and dismay. That huge and often prosperous class, damned as being in trade, usually were clever enough to keep their ungenteel origins a secret. There were splendid mansions springing up in the suburbs where shopkeepers lived. It was called "sinking the shop." The shopkeeper had the decency to pretend to be a gentleman once he shook the dust of central London from his boots. Miss Macleod must be aware of the social stigma of trade. Perhaps she was naïve.

"I would not talk about your father being in trade if you wish to make a society marriage," he said.

Fiona, who had turned back her gloves to eat, held up one small hand and ticked off two fingers. "Item one," she said. "I do not wish to marry. Item two, I do not wish to get on in society."

"Then what are you doing with the Tribbles?"

"Peace and quiet," said Fiona candidly. "It is always better to go along with what other people want to a certain extent."

"But every young lady wants to get married," he protested.

"My lord," said Fiona firmly, "I am very hungry and I cannot eat and answer questions at the same time."

"I beg your pardon," he said stiffly.

"Your apology is accepted," said Fiona calmly. "I shall tell you when I have eaten enough and then you may question me again."

He found himself becoming angry. But good manners prevented him from letting his anger show in his face or in his manner. She ate a large quantity of food, very daintily, but with amazing speed.

Then she put down her knife and fork, dabbed at her mouth with her napkin, took a sip of wine, and half-turned to him. "You may continue, my lord."

"Perhaps it would only be polite to give you a chance to ask *me* some questions," he said.

"Very well. Are you married?"

"No."

"Do you intend to marry?"

"No, Miss Macleod."

"Then we are two of a kind. How odd it is to meet someone who does not wish to marry either!"

"Not odd in a man. Very odd in a woman."

"I do not have to marry, you see."

"Meaning you are rich. Then why this charade?"

"Because I do not gain control of my money until I am married or reach the age of twenty-one." Fiona sighed. "Two years. Only two years to go."

"But what of love, Miss Macleod?"

"You are hardly in a position to talk about love, my lord." Fiona looked highly amused.

"Am I so ugly?" A tinge of resentment was beginning to show in his eyes.

"Of course not, my lord. On the contrary, you are handsome, reputed rich, and titled. Had you fallen in love, then you would have been married. You as yet know nothing about love, obviously."

He studied the elfin face which a short time ago had so enchanted him. He found her self-assured manner highly irritating. He thought he knew why she had been foisted off onto the Tribbles and it was nothing to do with trade. He had a longing to tease and annoy.

"But you are *so* wrong," he murmured. "I *have* been in love . . . madly."

There was a certain stillness about her, and then she asked, "Why did you not marry her?"

"My family were against it. Her name was Tabitha—I called her Tabby for short. She was like a little kitten, all sweetness and play."

"And what did your family find so monstrous about this paragon?"

"My Tabby was a tavern wench."

Fiona raised those odd and beautiful eyes of hers to his. "My dear Lord Peter," she said sorrowfully. "we are so much alike. I, too, have been in love."

"Odso?"

"Yes," said Fiona dreamily. "He was my aunt's footman, Charles. So divine. So tall and fair and handsome."

"Well," remarked Lord Peter tartly, "when you reach the great age of twenty-one, you can seek him out and marry him."

"Alas, I cannot. He is married. To a kitchen wench. They keep a hedge tavern. What of your Tabby?"

"Who?"

"The love of your life," said Fiona patiently.

"The same. When I reached my independence, I went to find her."

"Married?"

"Yes. To a . . . er . . . footman."

"But footmen are not allowed to marry."

"He left his employ and became a gamekeeper."

"What a most enterprising footman," giggled Fiona.

"You should not laugh," said Lord Peter severely, "I was heart-broken."

A smell of bergamot enveloped them and a genteel cough sounded in their ears. "Miss Macleod," said Effy Tribble, "the dancing has recommenced this age and your partners are looking for you."

Fiona got to her feet and Lord Peter rose as well. "Good evening, my lord," she said demurely, buttoning her gloves. "I shall no doubt not see you again this evening. It would surely be too much of a coincidence if one of my other partners had the vapours and surrendered his dance to you."

She smiled sweetly on him and moved away with Effy.

"Minx," said Lord Peter Harvard to no one in particular.

"Captain Freddy Beaumont was most particular in his attentions," said Amy as the Tribbles' rented carriage bore them homeward at three in the morning. She tried to read the expression on Fiona's face, but the dim light from the carriage lamps bobbing on their springs was not strong enough to illuminate the girl's face clearly.

"No doubt he will call tomorrow," said Effy brightly. "Such legs! Did you mark his legs, Fiona?"

"Yes, divine," said Fiona, stifling a yawn.

Effy flashed a look of triumph at Amy, who winked. How pleased the Burgesses would be to learn their niece was engaged before the Season even began.

Assuming that all was right and tight, they did not question Fiona any further.

The Tribbles found to their surprise when they reached their home in Holles Street that the house was in darkness and the door was locked. Effy banged at the knocker, but no one answered it.

"I have a key," said Amy, opening a reticule like a coal-sack and hoisting out a massive iron key, which she inserted in the lock. "I'll go downstairs and see what has happened to that lazy butler."

"No, no," said Effy weakly. "Too tired. So very tired. Time enough in the morning."

So the Tribbles went to bed unaware of the great revolution that had taken place in the servants' quarters during their absence, when Frank had returned to preach anarchy and to rouse the staff with the news that he had it on the best authority that the Tribbles did not intend to pay any wages on the next quarter-day.

Chapter 3

Oh, let us love our own vocations,
Bless the squire and his relations
And always know our proper stations!
—*Old Hymn*

INSPIRED BY FRANK, THE servants
had celebrated their rebellion with sev-
eral bottles of the best port. Had it not been for this
celebration, Amy would never have found out about the
rebellion because the sober servants would have been at
their posts when dawn broke and alcohol and excitement
would no longer fuel their brains. It had not been Frank's
nonsense of rebellion which had spurred them on, but his
shattering news that the Tribbles did not intend to pay
their wages come next quarter-day. But all had gone to
bed determined to have a long sleep, made longer by the
port they had drunk, and so by the time they all awoke,
frightened and wondering whether they had run mad,

Baxter, the Tribbles' lady's maid, had broken the news to Amy.

"What are you talking about, Baxter?" said Amy, glancing at the clock. It was seven in the morning. "Why did you wake me?"

"It's as I tell you," said Baxter with gloomy relish. "That second footman, Frank, he come back last night and he starts saying as how servants were the equal of their betters. Harris told him to go and boil his head. Then Frank says he has it on good authority that they're not going to be paid any wages. Says a society gentleman told him."

"Which society gentleman?"

"Well, mum, he says as how it was Lord Peter Havard."

Frank had feared they would not believe the words of a plain mister, however grand, and so had said the first titled name that had come into his head.

"Lud! And they believed him?"

"Yes, mum. Drank the port and sang vulgar songs, they did."

Amy lay back against the pillows and said in a flat, cold voice, "You are a strong woman, Baxter. Go to that butler, Harris, and drag him from his bed and bring him here."

Baxter's grim old face cracked into a smile. She rolled up her sleeves and made for the door. "Very good, mum."

"Wait a bit. Are all the servants involved in this rebellion?"

Baxter longed to lie and say Yes, but a strict religious upbringing would not let her do so. "That Yvette just laughed at them and wouldn't be no part of it," she said sulkily.

"Very well. Go and fetch Harris."

Amy climbed out of bed and wrapped her long flat figure in a man's dressing-gown and sat in a chair by the fire. She was annoyed but not very surprised. It was not unusual in a London household to find rebellion among the servants. Some servants terrified their masters and mistresses so much that a special agency for getting rid of unwanted servants had come into being. The only trouble with the agency was that they replaced the rebelling servants with their own creatures, who turned out to be even worse.

There came sounds of an altercation from the passage outside, then the door was pushed open and the butler, Harris, was thrust into the room. He was unshaven and half-dressed.

"Well, Harris?" demanded Amy, fixing the butler with a steely eye. "We have had the colonists' revolution in America, then the bourgeois revolution in France, and now I suppose you hope that the great servants' revolution of Holles Street will also figure in the history books."

"No, ma'am. It was just that Frank said as how Lord Peter Havard told him that we would not be getting any wages. I didn't listen to his other rubbish, ma'am, but we were furious at the thought of not being paid."

"Frank is a second footman. Why did a butler so readily believe the lies of a second footman?"

Harris looked at her miserably. How could he explain that the ground was there, that he, Harris, was ready to be impressed by Frank's tawdry finery and boasts of friendship with lords and talk of injustice? That most of the year he and other servants were grateful for their positions and served their masters well, but that there came the one day out of the three hundred and sixty-five when life seemed unnatural and unjust?

"Often we hear tales of staff not being paid their wages, ma'am," said Harris. "Often and often. We had no reason to disbelieve Frank."

"And where is Frank supposed to have met Lord Peter?"

Harris twisted uncomfortably.

"Come along, man. I assume he had leave to go out. Where did he say he was going?"

"He said his mother was poorly."

"His mother died five years ago," said Amy, who made it her business to know the backgrounds of the servants before she employed them. "So where did he meet Lord Peter—Lord Peter, who, I would like to point out, was at that ball I attended last night?"

Harris hung his head. "Don't know, ma'am," he said.

"A pox on ye, you whoreson!" shouted Amy, her temper snapping. "I've a good mind to send the lot of you packing and live up to the reputation you have created for me. Of course you are going to get paid. I shall give you one more chance. Get to your duties. But before you do that, send Frank to me . . . *now!*"

The staff were already going about their duties, white-faced and silent. They had been roused by the row between Baxter and Harris, and the full enormity of what they had done had struck them like a hammer-blow. Outside lay cold and menacing London, where the jobless starved in the streets.

But Frank had disappeared. His bed was empty and his trunk gone.

Mr. Desmond Callaghan was also roused early that morning. Frank came bursting into his bedchamber, with Mr. Callaghan's valet screaming in protest and hanging on to Frank's coat-tails.

"You got me in trouble," howled Frank. "I told them servants what you said and all was merry and they were all saying as how they'd sit tight and do no work for the Tribbles. Then this morning, that butler, Harris, was dragged from his room by the lady's maid, screeching and hollering, and the first footman and the rest look as if they've been struck by lightning and they start to run about the house like headless chickens, dusting and polishing as if their lives depended on it."

Mr. Callaghan waved his valet away and when the door was closed, he said sulkily, "I have no use for you, Frank. I have no doubt you told the servants it was I who said they would not be paid."

"No, I didn't," said Frank. "They wouldn't believe a plain mister, so I told 'em it was Lord Peter Havard."

Mr. Desmond Callaghan went a muddy colour. "You fool!" he hissed. "Those two harridans will tax Havard with it and he'll come looking for my blood. Get out of here."

"I can't," said Frank. "I've lost my job."

"Sent you packing, did they?"

Frank did not want to confess he had been too frightened to stay and find out. "Yes," he said.

"Well, I can't do anything for you. I've got to leave Town until I'm sure Havard isn't going to challenge me to a duel."

"But how will Havard challenge you to a duel when no one knows it was you that put me up to the whole thing?" said Frank.

Colour returned to Mr. Callaghan's cheeks. "Didn't split on me, eh?"

"No, sir."

"There's a good fellow. Sit down."

But Frank could not sit down. He had slept in his clothes and for some reason his tight trousers had become tighter.

"I don't suppose," said Mr. Callaghan slowly, "that you have any contact with anybody in that house in Holles Street."

"Yes," said Frank. "There's a chambermaid, Bertha, what's sweet on me."

Mr. Callaghan looked vaguely about him. He lived in

lodgings in Jermyn Street. A scrubbing woman did the heavy cleaning, and his valet and general factotum saw to the rest. There was scarcely room for a large footman. On the other hand, it would give him quite a cachet to have a six-foot-tall footman to follow him everywhere. And Frank had nowhere to go and so he did not need to be paid. Frank could also be encouraged to court this chambermaid and so find out what was going on in the house in Holles Street.

"You can stay as my footman," said Mr. Callaghan expansively. "Got your livery? Took it with you, I suppose."

"Yes, sir."

"Need to be changed a bit. New buttons. Gold shoulder knot would look good. Yes, you can stay."

Frank heaved a sigh of relief. The fact that the man lying in the bed in front of him had deliberately worked him up and lied to him, for Frank did not any longer believe a word about the Tribbles' not meaning to pay the servants' wages, was completely forgotten in a rush of gratitude. He knelt by the bed and kissed Mr. Callaghan's limp hand. There came a tremendous crack like a jib coming loose in a north-easter. Frank's trousers had split at last.

In the days that followed, Amy and Effy were to blame Frank for more than the servants' rebellion. If it had not been for Frank's nonsense, they would not have forgotten that one and all-important fact about Fiona—that in some way the girl disaffected any suitor on the point of proposing.

But then, it was not entirely Frank's fault. Neither Amy nor Effy expected Captain Freddy Beaumont to ask leave to pay his addresses so soon.

Amy had gone back to sleep, and was roused again at twelve noon by Baxter with the interesting information that the captain was in the drawing-room and desired to speak to one or both of the sisters.

"Get Effy!" cried Amy, throwing back the bedclothes. "And get Yvette to dress Fiona in something enchanting."

"I am perfectly well able to choose a gown for Miss Macleod myself," said Baxter huffily. "Those Frenchies—"

"Slut on you and your xenophobia," howled Amy. "Do as you are told!"

It took Amy a bare fifteen minutes to dress and go down to the drawing-room. But she did not feel the captain should state his business until Effy arrived on the scene, and so both the captain and Amy nervously drank glass after glass of wine and talked about horses.

Half an hour after Amy, Effy sailed in, trailing a great many gauze shawls.

"You look like a haunting," snapped Amy, who was bad-tempered with the strain of waiting.

"Forgive my sister," murmured Effy, holding out an arm bent like a swan's neck. The captain clicked his heels and bowed and kissed her hand.

"Now, ladies," he said. "I wish your permission to pay my addresses to Miss Macleod."

Rivalries forgotten, the sisters beamed at each other and then at the captain. He was so very handsome. It never crossed their minds that Fiona would not want him.

Effy rang the bell. When the first footman, Henry, answered the summons, Effy said grandly, "Pray tell Miss Macleod to present herself in the drawing-room."

"Yes, ma'am. Certainly, ladies. I shall go directly," babbled Henry, bowing so low his nose almost touched his knee.

Harris had not told the servants yet they were to stay,

43

knowing they would work doubly hard and that would impress the Tribbles with his own firm management.

In a little while, Fiona entered the room. The animation of the previous evening had gone. She looked delicate and pretty in a gown of figured muslin, but her large eyes were fathomless, great empty pools as they looked at the handsome captain.

"Captain Beaumont has something important to say to you," said Amy. "Come, Effy."

Both sisters left the room with their arms entwined around each other's waists.

"Do sit down, Captain," said Fiona in a voice as colourless as her eyes.

"Rather stand, Miss Macleod. Gawd! This will come as a surprise. But you struck me all of a heap at the ball last night. Right here!" exclaimed the captain, striking the region of his heart.

"Before you go on . . . ," began Fiona, but Captain Beaumont dropped to one knee in front of her and seized her hand.

"Be mine!" he cried. "For I cannot live without you. Oh, Miss Macleod, say you will be my bride."

"You do not know anything about me," said Fiona, gently disengaging her hand. "My father, while he lived, was in trade."

"Isn't everybody?" cried the captain gaily, although secretly he was rather shocked. Still, the man was dead, and Fiona was obviously too young and naïve to know that one did not talk about things like that in polite society.

"That is not all," said Fiona. "I am not a virgin."

The captain rose slowly to his feet and sat down in a chair facing her. "Miss Macleod, I . . . I . . . Gawd!"

"Yes, sir. I fear I lost my virginity two years ago."

"Who was the dastard?" cried the captain.

"Oh, no dastard. My aunt's footman, Charles. I loved him madly. I still do," said Fiona sorrowfully.

A tide of red swept up the captain's cheeks. He looked at Fiona with sorrowful admiration. "Gawd! Miss Macleod. Such honesty. I am a rich man. You could have fooled me. Your honesty makes me worship you."

"But you must realize," said Fiona with a tinge of irritation in her voice, "that you cannot marry me."

"Exactly," agreed the captain. "Believe me, ma'am, your secret is safe with me. If there is ever anything I can do . . . ?"

"I will let you know," finished Fiona. "Good day, my dear Captain Beaumont. Please do not disclose any of this to the Misses Tribble."

"Wouldn't dream of it," he said, seizing her hand again but this time working it up and down like a pump-handle. "Er . . . know it might be a misalliance, but can't you marry this footman? Make an honest . . . er . . . of you?"

"Alas, he married someone else," said Fiona. "I must take my shame with me to the grave."

"Damme," swore the captain, his black eyes gleaming with admiration. "I've a good mind to marry you after all!"

"Oh, no," said Fiona sadly. "It would be all right at first, don't you see, but later you would come to despise me."

The captain hesitated. He thought of his martinet of a father and his prim mother. "You may be right," he sighed. "Goodbye, Miss Macleod, and thank you for your honesty."

He nearly collided with the Tribble sisters as he left the drawing-room.

"Going so soon?" twittered Effy.

"Lud, yes," said the captain, all mad cheerfulness. "Got what I came for."

"Our congratulations," said Amy, surprised. "But

45

won't you stay? There is much to be discussed—marriage settlements, wedding . . ."

" 'Fraid you misunderstood, ladies," said the captain. "Came to get a recipe of that Scotch dish for m' mother. Haggis, that's it. Very tasty. Good for the spleen. Goodbye, ladies."

Strangled sounds of protest followed his hasty exit.

Amy and Effy walked slowly into the drawing-room. Fiona was standing by the window, looking vacantly out into the street.

"What is the meaning of this?" demanded Amy. "That man came to propose marriage and now he says he only called to get a recipe for haggis, whatever that is."

"It's a pudding made from minced offal and onions and cooked in a sheep's stomach," said Fiona.

"Listen, you trollop!" said Amy, advancing on Fiona with her fists clenched. "You can take your haggis and you can stuff it up your—"

"Mr. Haddon," announced the butler.

"Perhaps I am called at a bad time," said Mr. Haddon, looking from Amy's scarlet face to Fiona's blank one and then at Effy, who had begun to cry.

"No," said Amy heavily. "What fools we were not to listen to her uncle and aunt. Captain Freddy Beaumont came here and asked leave to pay his addresses to Fiona. He was only alone with her for a few minutes and then he leaves, swearing blind that all he had called for was a recipe for some Scotch muck."

Effy rallied and dried her eyes and blew her nose. "What did you say to him to put him off, Fiona?"

"I do not know," said Fiona. "I have the headache, and when I have the headache I cannot remember a thing."

"Go to your room," said Amy, controlling her temper with a great effort. "We will speak to you later."

Fiona curtsied to Mr. Haddon and left.

46

"You told me she had done this sort of thing before," said Mr. Haddon. "Did you not think to stay in the room with her while the captain made his proposal?"

"We had a contretemps with the servants," said Amy, "and I'm blessed if I didn't think anything other than the triumph of having secured such a splendid match for the girl."

"Trouble with the servants?" asked Effy. "What trouble?"

"Tell you later," said Amy. "What are we going to do about Fiona? I could whip her!"

Mr. Haddon leaned back in his chair and put the tips of his fingers together. "That is what the Burgesses would do. That, if I remember rightly, is what you told me they did do. No, we simply must find out what it was she said to the captain. I shall go and see him myself."

"Thank you," said Amy gruffly.

Effy fluttered up to Mr. Haddon, trailing wisps of gauze. "Oh, thank you," she breathed. "It is so wonderful to have a *gentleman* to help us."

After Mr. Haddon had left, the sisters decided to wait for his report before confronting Fiona again and trying to drag the truth out of her. At three in the afternoon, the gentlemen callers began to arrive. It was the custom for gentlemen to pay their respects the following day to the ladies they had danced with the night before. Most usually did not trouble to call in person but merely sent their servant, along with a card or a bunch of flowers. But with the exception of Lord Peter Havard, all the rest turned up at the Tribbles'. Fiona behaved like a model miss, chatting innocuously of this and that while the sisters sat and watched her with hot angry eyes.

By four o'clock, the last caller had gone and the sisters left Fiona in the drawing-room to play the piano while they retreated to the morning-room for a council of war.

They were rapidly coming to the conclusion that the Burgesses had been right and that there was something sly about Fiona when Harris, the butler, entered and informed the startled sisters that Lord Peter Havard was in the drawing-room, being entertained by Miss Macleod.

"And I'll bet the little minx is being as charming as possible to that crass waste of time," grumbled Amy, "Come along, Effy, and let's not go in for a moment. We'll listen at the door and find out what she says when we're not there."

Lord Peter had been discussing Fiona's aversion to marriage and teasing her about it. Fiona was about to interrupt when she heard a rustle of taffeta petticoats outside the door. "I have been practising a new piece for the pianoforte," said Fiona. "Allow me to play it for you."

"I should be charmed to hear it," said Lord Peter, but with some surprise at being so ruthlessly cut off in the middle of his monologue about marriage.

After ten minutes, Lord Peter wondered if he would ever be allowed to escape. He did not recognize the piece. It seemed very dull and endless. He shifted restlessly in his chair and then rose to his feet to go and turn the pages of music for her.

She was wearing a delicate flower perfume. Her head was bent over the keys and her neck was very white and fragile. He had to admit she intrigued him. He wondered if her total lack of interest in him was because of her father's disreputable background. Marrying a duke's son, albeit a younger one, might be considered flying too high. Then, as the dreary music tinkled on and on, he began to wonder seriously *why* people in trade were damned as being beyond the pale. He knew shopkeepers who were more gentlemanly and respectable than their clients. He himself gambled on the Stock Exchange. That was trade.

He was irritated to find himself possessed of ideas that were surely very old-fashioned. He deftly turned five pages at once so that Fiona found herself playing the last page.

"Oh, now you have spoilt my pretty piece," she said. "You have missed such a large bit of it. I shall start at the beginning again."

The sisters came into the room. Lord Peter noticed with surprise that they were looking at little Miss Macleod with dislike in their eyes.

"I am sorry you have been left alone," said Effy. "But I am sure you are just finishing your call."

Lord Peter bowed and took his leave.

That the Tribbles wanted to be rid of him was all too evident. He decided to forget about the infuriating Miss Macleod. He and his friends were holding a party back-stage at the opera and there were several very pretty opera dancers who would not dream of boring the handsome Lord Peter by playing dreary music.

Mr. Haddon came back about nine in the evening. He had had a difficult time finding Captain Beaumont. He sadly informed the sisters that Captain Beaumont stuck to his story. He had never proposed marriage. He only wanted that recipe.

"So what's to be done?" cried Effy.

"It is very important for your reputations to get this girl married off," said Mr. Haddon. "Another success would secure *your* success. I suggest therefore that one of you ladies remains here with Fiona while the other travels with me to Tunbridge Wells. If we can find some of Miss Macleod's previous suitors, then perhaps we can get them to tell us what it was she said to them."

"I feel like giving her a good thrashing," grumbled Amy.

"As you recall, she has been thrashed before, to no avail," said Mr. Haddon. "Tunbridge Wells it is. Now which of you will come with me?"

Effy looked at Amy, and Amy looked at Effy. Both longed to be the one. But Effy was afraid of the countryside. She hated trees and bushes, cows and fields with a passion. Hyde Park was the nearest to grass and trees that she was prepared to go. Besides, what had she to fear from Amy's being alone with Mr. Haddon? Poor Amy, with her flat chest and great feet.

"I feel Amy should go," she said meekly. "She is such an Amazon, and poor delicate little me would find the journey too, too fatiguing."

"Then that's settled," said Mr. Haddon. "Miss Amy, I feel we should leave tomorrow. There is no time to be lost."

Chapter 4

Walking about their grove of trees,
Blue bridges and blue rivers,
How little thought them two Chinese
They'd both be smashed to shivers.

—*Thomas Hood*

Despite the butler's secrecy, the staff at Holles Street soon found out from Barker that the Tribbles had no intention of dismissing them, and so they settled down to work like ordinary London servants and less like frightened slaves.

The Tribbles, like many of their kind, did not concern themselves with the lives of their servants. Strangely enough, unpopular employers were those who did. Servants left under the control of a butler, provided the butler was a reasonable man, could organize their lives free from interference and even occasionally gain some time off.

Harris was not a typical London butler in that he was small and fussy instead of being large and fat. He did his job competently, but he had a soft heart for the women servants, particularly for a certain pretty chambermaid called Bertha.

Not that Bertha would generally be accounted pretty for she had red hair, and since the prejudice against the Scots still ran deep, red hair was considered something of a defect, like having a hump or a squint. But Bertha had a neat figure and a roguish eye. Perhaps what had drawn her to the now ex-second footman, Frank, was that his sandy hair was classed in the same low category as red.

Frank knew that when the mistresses were gone from home, the lower servants were often allowed to emerge from the basement and take the air at the top of the area steps.

By assiduously watching the house, he was fortunate enough to see Bertha's jaunty cap and red curls emerging from the lower depths two days after Amy and Mr. Haddon had departed for Tunbridge Wells.

Mr. Callaghan had lent his new footman a domino and mask for his nightly spying activities. Ridottos were still popular, and so it was not an uncommon sight to see a masked man.

But when the muffled and masked figure of Frank crept up on her, Bertha let out a squeak of alarm.

"Shhh! It's me, Frank," whispered the footman.

"Oh, Mr. Frank. You did give me a turn," gasped Bertha. "Whatever happened to you?"

"I left before they could shove me off," said Frank with a swagger. "Walk a little with me, Bertha."

Bertha glanced nervously down the stairs. Through the barred and lighted window of the servants' hall, she could see Harris decanting port. That would take up all his attention for a bit.

"All right," she said. "But just a little way. You was wicked, Mr. Frank, to get us all so worked up. They're going to pay our wages, and they forgave us like the ladies they are."

"I could tell you a thing or two," said Frank darkly. "I'm working for a gentleman in Jermyn Street what was cheated out of his inheritance by them Tribbles."

"Never!"

"Fact!" Frank began to tell a highly false and dramatic story of a forged will and multiple intrigues, finishing up with the final whopper that his gentleman suspected the Tribbles had poisoned their aunt.

Betha turned white. "I'm going back to my mum in Shoreditch," she gasped. "I'm never going to stay in a house with murderers!"

Frank cursed under his breath. He needed Bertha to stay where she was. "They'll never touch you," he scoffed. "But my master is sweet on that Miss Macleod and fears for her. Why don't you find out when she goes out walking and leave a little note in that crack between the first and second steps?" This was where they had left little messages for each other in the past.

Bertha shivered and protested until he kissed her cheek and whispered that his master had promised him an independence should his, Frank's help amount to anything, and then Frank would be free to marry his Bertha.

There is nothing like a proposal of marriage to banish fear. Bertha's cheeks turned back to their usual healthy pink and her eyes glowed.

The very next day, Frank prized a slip of paper out of the crack at the top of the area steps. "Wokking in Park at 2," it said.

Triumphantly he returned to his master. But when Mr. Callaghan presented himself in the Park at two o'clock, it was to find Miss Macleod followed by that dragon, Bax-

53

ter, who had hated him so passionately when she had been lady's maid to the Tribbles' late aunt.

There was nothing for it but to beat a retreat. He cursed Frank roundly, blaming him for not having warned him about Baxter. Frank replied sulkily that he had not known where Baxter had been previously employed. He was ordered to return to Holles Street that night and try to get Bertha to do something to Baxter so as to put her out of commission.

Frank waited and waited, but there was no sign of Bertha. Effy, who had been out at the theatre, returned, and one by one the candles in the tall house were snuffed out. Frank was about to turn away when one of the little windows in the attic opened and Bertha leaned out.

She saw the muffled figure in the square waving to her and hesitated only a moment. She knew it was Frank, but she shared the room with three other maids and could not call out. She muttered an excuse that she was going out to the privy in the back garden, and ignoring the surprised remarks of the other maids to the effect that there was a perfectly good chamber-pot in the room, she pulled an old cloak over her night-gown and ran down the stairs.

Some of Frank's drunken preaching of the equality of Englishmen and women had stayed buried in Bertha's breast to give her courage. She knew she was defying Harris's orders, but Harris to a chambermaid *was* a member of the higher class and disobedience was a way of striking back. There were many Britishers, including Lord Byron and a great section of the Whig party, who admired Napoleon and cheered French victories. This heady atmosphere of liberty, equality, and freedom had infected even the London servants to a certain extent, which was why Frank's preaching had fallen on such fertile ground. Feeling as if she were storming the Bastille, Bertha unlocked the area door and crept up the stairs.

Frank's hissed instructions were quite simple. Bertha was to put some laudanum in Baxter's tea so that another maid or the footman would be sent with her when she went to the Park.

Now truly carried away by all the romance and secrecy, Bertha promised.

But it was another matter in the clear light of the following morning. Baxter was such a dragon that Bertha knew she could not possibly do it, even though it was one of her duties to take Baxter up her morning cup of tea.

Feeling like a very ordinary London chambermaid and not at all like a heroine of the revolution, Bertha pushed open the door of Baxter's bedchamber and went in and deposited the cup of tea, innocent of anything except tea-leaves, on the table beside Baxter's bed.

A dismal cough greeted her ears as Baxter came awake. Bertha turned round. Baxter's nose was red and her eyes were streaming. "Got a code," groaned Baxter.

Bertha immediately saw the chance of pleasing Frank while not harming Baxter. "Then you oughts to stay in bed," said Bertha.

"Miss wants to go walking in the Bark," said Baxter through her nose.

"Oh, you shouldn't do that," cried Bertha. "You could die of an inflammation!"

The chambermaid tripped off to Fiona's room and scratched at the door and went in. Fiona was awake and reading a morning newspaper. Bertha bobbed a curtsy and said breathlessly, "You must speak to Miss Baxter, miss. She has a terrible cold and ought to stay in bed. But she says as how she has to go to the Park."

Fiona climbed out of bed and pulled on a wrapper. "Nonsense," she said. "Henry, the footman, will do just as well."

And so it was that Mr. Callaghan had the pleasure of

seeing Fiona walking across the grass of Hyde Park accompanied only by a footman. He was so pleased that he even contemplated paying Frank some wages.

He waited until Fiona was about to walk past him and bowed low. Fiona inclined her head and walked on. Mr. Callaghan skipped in front of her and bowed again. Again, Fiona nodded. Mr. Callaghan darted off round a stand of trees to appear in front of her once more. Fiona stopped. "You are making yourself appear ridiculous, sir," she said calmly. "Pray do stop running about the Park like a March hare."

Mr. Callaghan flushed. He was wearing his newest bottle-green coat and his swansdown waistcoat. Surely the combination of both was enough to melt a heart of stone.

"I have seen you before," went on Fiona, scrutinizing this Pink of the Ton with uncomfortably shrewd eyes. "You seem to spend a great deal of your time in Holles Street."

"I confess it, madam. I confess. I watch and wait for even the slightest glimpse of you."

"Are you so deeply in debt?" asked Fiona with interest. Mr. Callaghan looked at her in a baffled way. But Fiona's train of thought was quite simple. Mr. Callaghan, she had quickly decided, spent a fortune on showy clothes. He wanted to know her; he probably wanted to marry her, having heard she was an heiress, and so he was now chasing her in the Park.

"I may as well add that I am never going to marry anyone," said Fiona.

"I could melt your heart," cried Mr. Callaghan. He clutched his heart and sank to one knee on the path in front of her.

"Shall I clear it away, miss?" asked Henry, surveying Mr. Callaghan with dislike.

"I do hope that will not be necessary," said Fiona. "Do rise, sir, and stop making a cake of yourself."

"Can I be of assistance, Miss Macleod?"

Fiona turned to face Lord Peter Havard, who was walking quickly towards her.

Mr. Callaghan leaped to his feet, his face aflame. "Dear me, Callaghan," drawled Lord Peter. He took out his quizzing-glass and walked around the embarrassed Fribble, scrutinizing his clothes. Then he gave a shudder. "I can think of nothing worse, Miss Macleod," he said, "than having such clothes thrust under one's nose on a sunny day."

"Are you insulting me?" cried Mr. Callaghan.

"My dear chap," said Lord Peter, "I am simply making an observation. Don't kill me. Kill your tailor."

Fiona to Lord Peter's disgust, suddenly gave Mr. Callaghan a warm smile. "I suggest, sir," she said, "that you ask my chaperones for permission to call. Good day to you."

Mr. Callaghan puffed out his buckram-wadded chest and flashed a smile of triumph at Lord Peter. "Thank you, Miss Macleod," he said. "I am honoured."

Fiona walked ahead, and Lord Peter fell into step beside her. Mr. Callaghan quitted the field of battle, feeling he had achieved a great deal for one day.

"Now why did you encourage the attentions of that creature?" demanded Lord Peter.

"I was sorry for him," said Fiona. "There I was, disliking him immensely and quite able with Henry's help to get shot of him, when you must needs step in and insult the poor little man, who has neither the physique nor the bottom to challenge you to a duel—a fact of which you were well aware. I fear you are a bully, Lord Peter."

"*I* thought I was being a knight errant," he said. "The next time I see you in distress, I shall turn the other way."

"Do that," said Fiona. "What are you doing in the Park, unmounted, and at this unfashionable hour? It is two o'clock, you know, not five o'clock."

"I like walking," said Lord Peter, "and I am not bound by the dictates of fashion."

"Perhaps. Yet why do you and the other gentlemen so slavishly follow the fashion set by Mr. Brummell? Gone are the days of silks and laces. Now you are all like wasps or crows."

"May I point out, Miss Macleod, that a lady *never* insults a man's dress."

"Which you just did. Poor Mr. Callaghan. He has a certain charm. Like a whipped and overclipped and scented poodle."

Fiona was wearing violet. Her eyes were violet too, he noticed despite his fury. He turned to walk away, and yet something made him turn back and continue to walk beside her. He remembered the party at the opera. What an orgy of champagne and breasts and thighs and dissipation! What would Miss Macleod think of him if she knew of his licentious behaviour?

"No," said Fiona, seemingly apropos of nothing, "I do not approve of rakes."

"Why?" he demanded, although he had received a sharp shock and wondered whether she was a mind-reader.

"Well, it *sounds* all right," said Fiona. "You know, dashing and dangerous. Understandable and forgivable in a very young man, but in an older man, say in his thirties, rather sad and immature."

Lord Peter Havard was thirty-three and he felt his feelings at that moment could only be relieved by slapping her hard. Controlling himself with an effort, he said, "You could not possibly even begin to understand. Men are different from women."

"Physically, yes. Mentally—how so?"

"Fall back apace," snapped Lord Peter over his shoulder to Henry. Then, as the footman obeyed, he said in a low voice, "Men have stronger passions."

"More guilty of lust, you mean," said Fiona airily.

"One of the seven deadly sins which you have never experienced?"

Fiona smiled but said nothing.

"Ah, the footman-lover. I had forgot."

"My feelings for that poor man were pure and good," said Fiona primly.

"Miss Macleod, if you wish the forthcoming Season to end in success, then I suggest you get your female trainers to teach you the art of flirting."

"In other words, I am to stop making myself thoroughly unpleasant to gentlemen such as you who hitherto have only known toadying and flattery? Walk on, my dear Lord Peter. Walk on. There is no need to endure more."

"I should not expect elegance from a tradesman's daughter."

"Cheap. Very cheap," commented Fiona. "You and your friends affect to despise trade. Miss Darsey, aged eighteen, was married amid floods of tears in St. George's t'other day to Baron Breadly, aged sixty-five. She is pretty and young and has a small dowry, he is old and ugly and rich. Now if that is not trading, what is? Go to any ballroom in London, my lord, and you will find us young ladies all up for sale to the highest bidder. Trade. And yet such as you dare to despise such as me."

"Enough! I never want to see you again."

"That is easily done. Come, Henry."

Rigid with anger, Lord Peter watched her walk away. Her pliant figure swayed slightly and, almost as if conscious of his gaze, she unfurled a lilac parasol as if to block it off.

It is not only young girls who live in fantasies of love and romance. Before setting out for Tunbridge Wells with Mr. Haddon, Amy Tribble had lain awake weaving rosy scenes and dreams about the forthcoming trip. Speaking glances were exchanged along with loaded sentences. Bosoms heaved with suppressed passion up till the final passionate kiss and . . . oh, glory, oh, wonder! . . . the very highlight of the fantasy was the entering the drawing-room in Holles Street hand in hand with Mr. Haddon to break the news to Effy of their engagement. By the time an exhausted Amy climbed into Mr. Haddon's travelling carriage, she could hardly understand why that gentleman was behaving in much the usual way, for in her mind Amy had kissed him, lain with him, married him, quarrelled with him, and had even run off with another man so as to create a passionate reunion.

She would have been thoroughly distressed had she known that the practical Mr. Haddon had put her strange and weary behavior down to those odd feelings which seemed to beset ladies of a certain age.

But soon the dream Mr. Haddon faded from Amy's mind to be replaced by the present real one. To Mr. Haddon's relief, Amy appeared to become her usual practical self, and by the time they reached Tunbridge Wells, they were once more the best of friends.

Amy was reluctant to approach the Burgesses because she felt to do so would advertise failure. But Mr. Haddon said it might take days, gossiping and questioning about the famous spa, to find out the names of any of Fiona's previous suitors.

Shortly after they had booked in at a comfortable inn, they found themselves in the Burgesses' chilly drawing-room. A reluctant spring was blossoming outside the windows, but inside it felt like perpetual winter. No fire was lit, and little pieces of soot decorated the orange crepe paper that decorated the empty hearth.

"I assume you have failed" was Mrs. Burgess's opening remark.

"Not a bit," said Amy. "But if we are to do our best for Fiona, we must find out what she said to her previous suitors."

"You look a strong woman," said Mrs. Burgess acidly. "Try the birch."

Amy's dislike for Fiona fled. Poor girl. It was no wonder she was a trifle sly and odd. "We think it would be better if we could question some of her previous suitors," said Amy. "Perhaps if you could let us have their names . . . ?"

"Never!" said Mr. Burgess. "The shame of it all. The humiliation. No. We do not want to rake over the cinders of the past."

"But surely you must see the wisdom of Miss Tribble's request?" pleaded Mr. Haddon.

"No. Go away," said Mrs. Burgess.

"In that case," said Amy, sending up a silent prayer that Effy would forgive her if her plan did not work, "we may as well return your money and Miss Macleod to you as soon as possible."

"You will carry on and do what you promised," said Mrs. Burgess wrathfully.

"We cannot proceed unless you give us the name of at least one suitor," said Amy firmly.

Mr. and Mrs. Burgess exchanged glances. Mrs. Burgess rang the bell and when the parlourmaid answered it, she said, "Mary, take this lady and gentleman to the library. We wish a private discussion, Miss Tribble."

Mr. Haddon and Amy had to wait nearly a quarter of an hour before being summoned back.

61

"Mr. Willox of Courtney Hall, two miles out on the London road," said Mrs. Burgess stiffly.

Mr. Willox turned out to be a pleasant gentleman with a square face and steady grey eyes. To Amy's questions, he shook his head and swore he had never proposed marriage to Fiona.

Seeing that Amy was about to lose her temper, Mr. Haddon suggested she should go and admire Mr. Willox's excellent gardens. Once they were alone, he said mildly to Mr. Willox. "I fear the ladies never quite understand how sensitive and honourable we gentlemen are. But you must realize that if Fiona has been turning down proposals and then swearing her suitors to secrecy, this is something we should know. If you have any affection in your heart left for her, please tell me. We cannot help the girl otherwise."

"You mean I'm not the only one?" asked Mr. Willox, scratching his fair hair in bewilderment.

"I fear not."

"Do you mean," said Mr. Willox, growing visibly angry, "that she was lying to me?"

"That would appear to be the case."

"Well, I'm dashed if I can believe she would. . . . The long and the short of it is that I did propose marriage and Miss Macleod told me that she had galloping consumption and was not like to live very long. I wanted children, of course, and so I said in that case I must withdraw my proposal. She made me swear not to tell anyone I had proposed, but, dash me, when I saw her uncle and aunt outside the door, I could only babble some nonsense at them and take to my heels."

"Was there anyone else courting her about that time?"

"There was the Honourable James Fordyce at Just Hall, that's the other side of the town, but I don't know if he was serious about her."

This time Amy agreed to stay at the inn while Mr. Haddon went to interview Mr. Fordyce. When Mr. Haddon returned, Amy listened eagerly to his news. Fiona had told Mr. Haddon that her mother had died mad, that there was madness in the family, and that she could never marry.

"So she must hate the very idea of marriage!" exclaimed Amy. "Why, I wonder?"

"There must be some ladies who do not wish to marry," pointed out Mr. Haddon.

"No," said Amy. "There ain't a single one."

Mr. Callaghan learned that Effy was to visit an old friend one afternoon. The butler had, of course, been told not to admit any visitors, but Mr. Callaghan thought he would try his luck. Harris was, after all, not the butler who had seen him forcibly ejected from the house by Miss Amy the previous year.

He presented his card barely five minutes after Effy had left. Harris bowed and said Miss Macleod was not receiving callers, but eyed the huge posy which Mr. Callaghan held in front of him with a sympathetic eye.

Mr. Callaghan pressed a guinea into the butler's hand and murmured he was sure Miss Macleod would be more than happy to receive him.

Harris took the card and retreated up the stairs to the drawing-room. Fiona was restless and bored. Her days of misery and bullying under the Burgesses' rule had at least made her appreciate every free moment. But now she felt she had too much time on her hands and too little to do. Obscurely, she blamed Lord Peter. What an irritating man! She had felt quite comfortable before she met him. At first she did not recognize Mr. Callaghan's name. Then she remembered him as the Fribble from the Park. Although there was very little chance of Lord Peter's ever finding out about Mr. Callaghan's visit, Fiona felt she was somehow scoring a point by agreeing to see this freak of fashion.

Mr. Callaghan came in and handed her the bouquet and bowed and scraped and bowed and scraped until Fiona became heartily tired of curtsying in return.

"Pray sit down, sir," begged Fiona, already regretting her impulse to see him.

"Lady of my heart," began Mr. Callaghan, his pale eyes flashing fire. "I have written a poem in your honour."

He unrolled a long piece of parchment.

"How kind," said Fiona faintly. "May I not read it later?"

"No, no. 'Twill melt your heart. Hark!" Mr. Callaghan proceeded to read.

> *"Fiona, walking in the Park*
> *Doth make my pulses race.*
> *I do not pursue her for a lark*
> *Or for the fun o' the chase.*
> *I sigh, I pant . . ."*

He broke off. There were sounds of arrival from the hall downstairs.

"Do go on, Mr. Callaghan," said Fiona, her eyes full of tears of suppressed laughter.

"No, no, better leave." Mr. Callaghan rolled up the parchment and rushed to the door. He scampered past Amy, who was mounting the stairs, and she turned with a cry of rage. Quick as a flash, Amy seized a large willow-pattern plate from a table on the landing and hurled it down the stairs after Mr. Callaghan's retreating figure.

But he nipped through the door, which the butler was still holding open. The plate sailed over his head and crashed in pieces on the cobbles of the road outside.

Amy strode into the drawing-room. "What was that piece of garbage doing here? And where's Effy?"

"Miss Effy is making a call and Mr. Callaghan met me the other day in the Park and so came to call."

"Met you in the . . . ? Where's Baxter? *She* would never have let such a piece of shite near you!"

A flicker of amusement shone in Fiona's eyes. "Do you train all your charges to emulate your highly colourful vocabulary, Miss Amy?"

Amy had the grace to blush. "Sit down, Fiona," she said wearily, "and I'll tell you about Mr. Desmond Callaghan." And so Amy proceeded to tell Fiona how she and Effy had been so poor and at their wit's end but how they had hoped Mrs. Cutworth, their aunt, would leave them her fortune in her will. Then, went on Amy, they found that Mr. Callaghan, no relation, had been paying court to the old lady and so she had left him everything in her will. "Everything" had turned out to be nothing but bad debts, and Mr. Callaghan, noticing the Tribbles' new-found comfortable circumstances, had assumed that they had cheated Mrs. Cutworth before her death out of jewels and money that now rightly belonged to him.

"Whereas," interrupted Fiona, "you in fact obtained money from bringing out girls such as myself?"

"Precisely."

"And if I do not marry, do you lose the money paid to you by my aunt and uncle?"

"No," said Amy, "but we stand to lose a reputation. We fail with you and we may not get another for next Season."

"Trade," said Fiona mournfully. "It's all trade."

65

"And on the subject of marriage . . . oh, I hear Effy. Not a word about Callaghan. No need to upset her. He won't come round again."

It took Effy some time to settle down. Questions, sly questions, as to how Amy had fared with Mr. Haddon seemed to be of more interest to Effy than anything to do with Fiona. At last, she seemed reassured nothing of a tender nature had taken place between the two, and turned her eyes inquiringly on Fiona.

"Yes," said Amy grimly. "Now sit there, sister, and hear what I have learned about Fiona and marriage!"

Chapter 5

Those smiling matrons are appraisers sly,
Who regulate the dance, the squeeze, the sigh,
And each base cheapening buyer having chid,
Knock down their daughters to the noblest bid.

The Marriage Market, *Anonymous*

"SO," FINISHED AMY, "WE have it that you told the one you were consumptive, t'other you were like to go mad; so what did you tell the brave captain?"

Fiona sat very still, remembering the enormity of what she had told the captain. Better to lie. "I merely said I did not want to marry him, and that would he please not tell anyone he had proposed, because I should be in trouble."

"What ails you, girl?" cried Amy. Certain dark, half-remembered scandals came back to her. "Are you," she said, staring hard at the clock, "in the way of . . . er . . . disliking men?"

"Oh, no," said Fiona, and with a sudden flash of spirit.

"Have you considered that I might not have considered any of my suitors suitable?"

"Yes, I did consider that," said Amy. "So why not say so before they reach the point of declaring themselves?"

"Mrs. Burgess," said Fiona—the sisters noticed again that she hardly ever said my "aunt"—"does not allow for tender feelings. The size of the man's bank balance is all that matters. As long as she was kept in doubt that there ever had been a proposal, then there was no danger of her forcing me to accept."

"But there's more, isn't there?" said Effy quietly. "You hate marriage. I feel it."

Amy snorted in disdain, but to her surprise Fiona said simply, "Yes."

"Tell us why, dear," said Effy. "We shall not betray any confidence, but it is important that we know. If for some reason marriage is so repugnant to you, then we shall have to come to terms with that, and perhaps help you get through the time until you gain your inheritance."

"Effy—that would *ruin* us!" cried Amy.

"I think Fiona's happiness is all that matters," said Effy quietly. "Our needs must come second."

Shaken rigid by her sister's unusual fit of nobility, Amy felt silent and looked pleadingly at Fiona.

"All right," said Fiona. "I'll tell you.

"I was brought up in a very old house in Aberdeen. There is little privacy in a Scottish household. The servants are more family friends than servants and are allowed to say what they think. People do not hide family rows from servants—in fact, they often allow them to take sides. And so it was in my home. I think Mother and Father must have hated each other deeply. They were always rowing and quarrelling and the servants would shout and quarrel as well. I often wondered why I had no brothers or sisters, but I learned all too soon. Father was broad-spoken—blunt—and Mother would not allow him in her bedchamber. She said she had nigh died giving birth to me and would not risk death a second time." Fiona put her hands over her face. "The rows and abuse went on and on and on. I felt guilty. I felt I was somehow to blame. The children of the other families were either too good for me or not good enough, in my parents' opinion, and so I had no one to play with. My one friend was Ian, a servant. He would show me the nests of birds, how to make dolls out of clothes-pegs, how to fish . . . oh, all sorts of things. I loved him dearly. I was twelve and he was, I suppose, about thirty. My parents were away visiting one afternoon and he took me off into the country to look for a badgers' set. We stayed away longer than we intended, and when we returned, it was to find my father home and in a towering passion. Ian had kept our friendship secret, but some of the other servants knew of it, and they talked. My father accused him of all sorts of filthy things, without mincing his words. Ian was dismissed. A doctor was called in to examine me to make sure I was still a virgin. I shall never forget the humiliation—the disgust. Ian was a good man and sorry for me, but they could not understand that.

"When my parents died and I was sent south, I could barely mourn them. I was too excited at the thought of a new, free life. You have met my aunt and uncle. They are childless, and brought me up as they saw fit. But they wanted rid of me as soon as possible and made it plain it was my duty to accept the first suitable man who proposed. I am not strong, but I knew I would take any amount of beatings rather than marry. Marriage is a sham, a deception, a vile trade which has nothing to do with love or romance. I want no part of it."

She fell silent. The Tribbles looked at her in dismay while both wondered desperately what to do. They had been prepared to take on wild girls, spoilt girls, even ruined girls, but never had they envisaged trying to cope with a girl who hated and feared the very idea of marriage. And to think they had been bored and irritated with Fiona because she seemed to need no schooling whatsoever.

"There are good marriages," said Amy quietly. "I know it is hard for us women, and many of us must take what comes. But you are an heiress and can hope for compatibility and love. We won't force you into anything."

It was Effy who spoilt things, Effy, who had only been pretending to be altruistic to get Fiona to talk. While Fiona had been speaking, Effy had been locked in a nightmare fantasy of cold and poverty. She and Amy were just entering the workhouse with their meagre belongings; the tall iron gates clanged behind them, the poor shivering wretches in the workhouse were crowding round, grinning furtively and greedily eyeing the bundles the sisters carried with them. "No!" screamed Effy. "I cannot bear it. This is all we have left. Do not take it from us."

Fiona looked shocked, but Amy, who was used to her sister's fantasizing, groaned aloud and went and put an arm about Effy's shoulders. "Do not exercise yourself so much, Effy," she said gruffly. "We can always sell this house and move to a cottage in the country."

"I hate the country. I loathe it," said Effy, beginning to sob. "Bad drains and peasantry and genteel poverty and nasty-smelling candles and undisciplined animals in the fields who ought to wear *drawers!*"

To Amy's added distress, Fiona began to cry as well. "You are s-so kind," she wailed. "No one but Ian has ever been so kind to me before. Oh, I *shall* try to think of marriage, my dear Miss Amy and Miss Effy. Only dry your eyes. I am selfish and wicked."

Amy strode to the window and glared out and then

scrubbed her eyes with the back of her hand. "No need to sacrifice yourself," she said.

"I won't sacrifice myself," said Fiona. "I shall choose someone highly suitable and you will be covered in glory. Provided I choose a gentleman who is rich enough not to want my money, may I choose whom I please? That is the only stipulation I will make."

"Of course!" cried Effy, her tears drying like magic.

"Certainly," said Amy with a broad grin. "You can't have anyone in mind at the moment."

Fiona stood up. She had just decided never to tell lies again. But surely the Tribbles deserved just one little white lie to make them happy. And she did so much want them to be happy. "Yes, I do know someone," she said.

"Who!" demanded the sisters in unison.

"Lord Peter Havard."

"Oh, lud," said Amy.

"Not suitable, dear," said Effy. "The man has no interest in anything other than roistering and womanizing. Forgive me for speaking so plain."

"You agreed, you promised, that I might have the man of my choice," said Fiona stubbornly, disappointed that they had not hailed her declaration with relief. After all the trouble she had given them, she had been so sure they would have greeted the idea of marriage to anyone with delight.

Effy opened her mouth to speak, but Amy flashed her a warning glance. "We will discuss it later," she said in a milder tone. "I think we should all have a glass of champagne to restore our nerves."

A look of friendliness and happiness showed on Fiona's glowing face as she sipped her champagne; trepidation and worry on the sisters' side. What were they to do with the girl? It was wonderful to see her looking so happy. What would happen to her when Lord Peter ignored her, as he had ignored so many young misses in previous Seasons? Or worse? If Lord Peter was interested enough in Fiona to get his parents to invite her to that ball, then he might break her heart. And the sisters had promised Mr. and Mrs. Burgess to steer Fiona clear of Lord Peter.

When Fiona at last rose and said she was going to her room, the sisters could hardly wait for her to leave so they could discuss this new problem. No sooner had Fiona left than Mr. Haddon was announced and stood bewildered before a barrage of explanations about cruelty, marriage, and Lord Peter.

In his usual way, he sat down patiently and listened until he had the full story.

"I think it would be a dangerous thing to cross the poor girl at the moment," he said at last. "Besides, are you not worrying overmuch? Lord Peter Havard? He is too interested in sport and curricle-racing and every frivolity the fringes of the Season has to offer to pay attention to a young miss whose father hailed from the middle classes. I have noticed furthermore that Fiona has an oddly direct approach when speaking to gentlemen, even such elderly gentlemen as myself. She does not know how to flirt. Now, perhaps it is this . . . er . . . farouche manner of hers which has caught Lord Peter's interest, if it has been caught. She needs schooling. Oh, I know she has all the ladylike accomplishments such as dancing, water-colour-ing, and pianoforte-playing to perfection. But give her a little schooling in flirting and genteel conversation to turn her into a regular young lady like all the other young ladies and you may see his lordship's interest die. Correct young ladies attract correct young gentlemen. Eccentric ladies do not."

"So I had noticed," said Effy with a sly look at Amy, who coloured angrily and turned her head away.

"I would not, however, tell her why you are training

her in the art of flirtation," said Mr. Haddon. "Rather tell her that good behaviour gives rakes such as Lord Peter thoughts of marriage."

Mr. Haddon felt rather guilty when he left. But he felt he had to give the sisters something to work on. There was, however, a quality about Fiona that the sisters did not seem to have noticed. She was sensuous and passionate. It was in every movement of her body, in the turn of her head, in the occasionally caressing look in her odd eyes. But such things he, as a gentleman, could not discuss with two spinster ladies like the Tribbles.

Mr. Desmond Callaghan sat slumped in a wing-chair in his lodgings and stared moodily at the fire. "That Miss Amy is a Tartar, sir," said Frank, who sat in a corner polishing a pair of his master's boots. "No wonder she never married. Miss Effy's another matter. Ever so sweet she is and very pretty for an old lady. 'S funny, but all them two talk about is hopes of marriage. You'd think they'd have given up a long time ago."

"Anyway," said Mr. Callaghan, who had only been half-listening, "I don't see how I'm going to get near Miss Macleod again. The duns are a pest and my tailor has had the cheek to demand payment. I don't know what tradesmen are coming to these days. Maybe I'd better go back to chasing rich old women. I'm a dab hand at that. Didn't I get that old frump, Cutworth, to make out her will to me? It should have worked if those Tribbles hadn't cheated her out of everything before she died."

"Why don't you try your hand with Miss Effy?" asked Frank.

"You stupid lummox. I—"

Mr. Callaghan's mouth fell open as he stopped talking and turned over what Frank had said in his mind.

"Damme, but you might have it," he said. "Where do they go tonight?"

"Nowheres I know of," said Frank. "But Bertha says that everyone's going to that poet's, you know, Lord Aubrey."

"When?"

"Friday night. He's by way of being a distant relative of that old stick, Haddon, who's always hanging around Holles Street. Ladies are mad to meet him. Wrote some silly poem called *The Gypsy Baron*."

"Get me a copy," said Mr. Callaghan, "and then find out where I can come across Aubrey."

Lord Aubrey, like Lord Byron, had woken up one morning to find himself famous. The poem had actually been written by his sister, who had died two years before. Lord Aubrey had found the poem while going through her effects. He had taken it to a bookseller with the vague idea of selling it, but with no thought of claiming it as his own work. The shrewd bookseller, although thinking the poem not very good, knew that it could catch a market established by Lord Byron's *Corsair*. He praised Lord Aubrey for his brilliance, his talent, and offered him a generous sum for it. No one had ever called the beautiful but dull-witted Lord Aubrey clever before. He cheerfully took on the role of author. The long poem, a Gothic affair rather like one of Mrs. Radcliffe's novels in verse, was published. The critics tore it to shreds, but the ladies loved it. Lord Aubrey was fêted and petted as he had never been before. He dressed the part, tousled his fair hair into artistic disarray, and cultivated a smouldering look. He was sitting in his club, practising this look, when Mr. Callaghan found him.

Mr. Callaghan produced a leather-bound copy of the

poem and begged Lord Aubrey to sign it. Mr. Callaghan then sat down and quoted long extracts from it, which he had cleverly inked on his cuffs in case his memory ran out. Lord Aubrey was enchanted. He expansively invited Mr. Callaghan to a "little fork supper" he was having on Friday and Mr. Callaghan left flushed with success, his only worry being that Amy Tribble might throw the supper at him when she saw him.

Of the three ladies who set out from Holles Street on Friday night with Mr. Haddon, only Fiona was not particularly thrilled at the idea of meeting the great poet. She had read a copy of *The Gypsy Baron* and thought it quite terrible. She also wondered why she had told her chaperones that she wanted to marry Lord Peter. She had walked in the Park, but he had not been there, she had attended the opera, but he had been absent. Absence did not make the heart grow fonder. Fiona was basically practical enough to know that rakes did not reform. Lord Peter, who had seemed a stimulating adversary to cross swords with only a few days before, now seemed a bad-tempered, self-indulgent man who cared for nothing but idleness and pleasure.

She was not happy with the gown she was wearing, which had been chosen by the sisters rather than Yvette. It was one she had brought with her from Tunbridge Wells, a dainty, fussy affair of white muslin with a small sprig, a high neckline, and only two flounces at the hem.

She had promised the Tribbles she would remember her lessons. Amy, dressed as a man, had acted the gallant while Effy had stood on the sidelines, gently giving instructions on how to flirt. Fiona was anxious to please these two kind ladies and did her best, but it was very hard not to burst out laughing at Amy's horsehair side-whiskers and old-fashioned tie-wig. She was to confine her conversation to gushing praise of the poet's work, to the weather, and to genteel and mild gossip about members of society. Miss Harrison-Jones had recently married Sir Edward Trench. The bride had worn a veil. Would this bring bridal veils back into fashion? Also, more Fashionables were being married in church rather than in their drawing-rooms. "No, no, Fiona," Amy had admonished. "You are not to say you think it is a sign of a religious revival. You must say that churches are very pretty places in which to marry. Never talk about religion, even on Sundays, and do not, under any circumstances, mention Jesus Christ. He is not at all fashionable. Society does not like that bit about the eye of the needle, you know. And do not ever mention politics. It is to be assumed you are Tory. But ladies know nothing of politics. Nor do you mention the war in the Peninsula. It does not exist as far as you are concerned. A correct gentleman will not talk of those things either. A correct gentleman should be able to converse about the best place to buy gloves and interesting topics like that."

Lord Aubrey lived in a house in Bruton Street, which had been comfortable, conventional, and bookless until he became famous. He had read that a library was being offered at auction and had bought it before the auction by private contract. He had then sent all the books—without looking at them—to the bookbinder with instructions that the bindings were to be as rich and varied as possible. The works were of a somewhat miscellaneous character— old directories, poems by young ladies and gentlemen, ready reckoners, Dudridge's *Expositor,* Hints on Etiquette, two hundred Minerva Press novels, triplicate copies of some twenty books on cookery, the art of war, charades, Cudworth's *Intellectual System;* books of travels, Bibles, prayer-books, plays; Enfield's *Speaker,* and Burn's *Ecclesiastical Law.* But since Lord Aubrey only looked at the glowing bindings in their carved oak bookcases and never examined the contents, he was well pleased with the effect and felt more than ever like a man of intellect.

It was that irritating fashion of Regency notables to ask many more people than the house could comfortably hold in the hope that the social columns the next day would give the affair that highest of accolades, "a sad crush." Mr. Callaghan at first despaired of ever finding Miss Effy. People stood about, balancing plates of food and glasses, all jammed up against each other and barely able to move, let alone eat or drink. The literary luminaries of London society were conspicuous by their absence; Lord Aubrey feared being asked too many searching questions about art and literature. He enjoyed talking to the ladies, who flattered him and courted him.

He was greatly taken by Miss Fiona Macleod. She was exactly his idea of what a young miss should be. She talked about the weather, inclement, the difficulty of wearing gloves, getting them to wrinkle in the right manner, and weddings—did Lord Aubrey think church weddings were becoming fashionable again?

Lord Aubrey knew himself to be beautiful, but did not like any competition from the gentle sex. He liked the very quietness of Fiona's appearance, her slate-coloured hair, and her no-colour eyes, which he considered a good foil for his own golden hair, large pansy-brown eyes, and tall, elegant figure. He was wearing a loose-flowing tartan silk scarf, knotted negligently about his throat, instead of a cravat, and a royal-blue velvet coat with sapphire-and-gold buttons.

While he talked to Fiona, Amy stood on tiptoe to watch Fiona's behaviour. "Doing well," she muttered to Effy. "Very well. Aubrey's a fool, but pleasant and kind and rich. Just the ticket. Sad crush, but the Westphalian ham's good. I'm going to fight my way through the crowd and get some more."

Effy looked about her. "Where is Mr. Haddon? He could fetch it for you."

"He's lost in the crowd somewhere," said Amy. "Quite capable of feeding m'self."

She shouldered her way off.

The minute Amy had gone, Effy wanted to call her back. She felt ready to faint. Elbows jabbed into her back, hot bodies pressed against her, voices beat upon her ears.

She turned to escape and found herself looking up into the highly painted features of Mr. Desmond Callaghan. She gave a little cry of distress and tried to back away.

"Miss Tribble," he cried. "You are so white! Let me clear a path for you. There is a quiet place by the windows where you may get some fresh air."

Effy felt too weak to refuse. Normally, Mr. Callaghan would have been toadying and smiling to the important guests and would not have dreamt of shoving a path through them. But desire for revenge and desire for money stiffened his spine, and Effy soon found herself standing by the open windows at the back of one of the saloons with a refreshing breeze fanning her pale cheeks.

Mr. Callaghan felt the gods were on his side. On a table in the bay in which they stood was a small table holding a bottle of champagne and some glasses. He deftly poured two and handed one to Effy, who was eyeing him as if he were a snake.

"Please do not look at me so, fair one!" cried Mr. Callaghan. "It goes right to my heart. All those dreadful things I said to you! Please forgive me. But you must admit, Mrs. Cutworth let us all down."

Effy smiled at him in a tentative way. His eyes were glowing with warm admiration and he had called her "fair one." Feeling guilty, she looked about for Amy but could see no sign of her. "I accept your apology," said Effy, "but

78

you must admit, it did seem odd, you courting Mrs. Cutworth. It is not as if you were a relation."

"I was sorry for her," said Mr. Callaghan. "I was visiting relatives in Streatham and happened to come across her when I was walking on the Common. She invited me to tea and begged me to call again, saying she was lonely."

"But I thought Aunt was bedridden these past six years or more," exclaimed Effy.

"Mrs. Cutworth often took the air in a Bath chair on the Common. You can ask your maid, Baxter, whether I speak the truth or not. I had no intention of trying to get her money. Do believe me, my delicate and beautiful Miss Tribble. But I must say when I found I was her sole heir and she had left me nothing but debts, I lost all reason. The duns were pressing me and life was hard. Can you understand?"

"Oh, yes," sighed Effy, remembering their own too recent poverty.

"I felt I had been cheated and I accused you—oh, my shame!—of having taken her money and jewels. How can I make up for my terrible rudeness? When I saw you there with your beautiful silver hair shining in the candle-light and looking so fragile, like a crushed flower, my heart went out to you."

A slow feeling of delicious warmth started to grow inside Effy. It seemed such a long time since any man had paid her compliments. Mr. Callaghan, who only recently had seemed such a pathetic figure of fun with his tight lacing and ridiculous clothes, now seemed almost handsome. When a man looks at a lady with a world of admiration in his eyes, it is very hard for her to consider him a poor creature.

"I have already forgiven you," said Effy. fluttering her lamp-blackened eyelashes. "Do not distress yourself further."

"Alas, if only your sister would be so womanly—so forgiving. But I feel she hates me."

Effy felt a little uncomfortable. Amy would indeed be in a towering rage if she knew that her sister were even exchanging two words with the enemy. Amy had not yet told Effy of Mr. Callaghan's call on Fiona. Mr. Callaghan, studying her expressive face, decided he had better explain his call.

"I have another confession to make," he said, smiling ruefully and, he hoped, boyishly into Effy's eyes. "Did your sister tell you that I called on Miss Macleod?"

Effy's eyes grew hard. "No, she did not."

"You see, I needed some excuse to see you again. I knew I might be taken as just another of Miss Macleod's suitors, although I have no interest in the girl. Too immature." He looked down modestly. "I had been watching the house, you see, and knew your sister was absent, but unfortunately, I did not know that you, too, were gone from home."

"Mr. Callaghan," said Effy firmly, trying to hang on to the remains of her common sense, "I cannot believe that a young and fashionable man like yourself could be in the slightest bit interested in an old woman like me."

"Old! How can such monstrous lies escape your fair lips. Old! Look in your glass and you will see what I see. Your gentleness, your delicacy of movement. The young misses of today are too farouche, too hurly-burly."

Effy always prepared for a social outing in the dimmest of candle-light. She remembered herself as she had looked in her glass before she had set out that evening, with the smoky, greenish glass washing away all wrinkles. Every spinster of fifty, however sensible, has the soul of a seventeen-year-old virgin. Effy's heart beat quicker. Her vanity had stopped her from seeing her own proper image in the glass, and now her vanity changed the

80

weak and shifty Mr. Callaghan into a dashing and hand-some cavalier.

Several glasses of champagne and some heady compliments later and Effy, feeling like the heroine of one of her favourite romances, had agreed to meet Mr. Callaghan in St. James's Park the following afternoon at three o'clock.

While Effy was absorbed in the attentions of her new beau, Amy was at the far end of a chain of saloons, chatting happily to Mr. Haddon. She had him all to herself and she did not care what Effy was doing or, for that matter, Fiona. Mr. Haddon was talking about his experiences in India and Amy was hanging on his every word. And Mr. Haddon, who was often damned as a funny, dry old stick, was blossoming in front of the best audience he had ever had. He did think at one point that they should be searching in the crush for Fiona to find out what she was up to, but Amy had told him all about the girl's revelations and how good and affectionate she had become, and so he eased his conscience with the thought that Miss Macleod was probably at no risk from anyone.

Fiona was trying hard to please, but she was becoming heartily bored with Lord Aubrey, who showed no signs of leaving her side. She felt small and insignificant. She wished Amy had not overridden Yvette's choice of gown. Fiona knew that the white muslin she was wearing made her look washed out. She suddenly felt she could not bear Lord Aubrey one minute longer, and with a cry of dismay said that one of the flounces of her gown needed mending and excused herself, thrusting her way through the press with an energy as great as that previously demonstrated by Mr. Callaghan. She made her way down to the hall and into an ante-room reserved for the ladies. There she sat down wearily on a stool in front of a looking-glass and fiddled with her hair and powdered her nose and tried to summon up courage to plunge back into the crush.

With a little sigh, she stood up and went back out into the entrance hall. Lord Peter Havard, who had just arrived, was swinging his cloak from his shoulders. The two stared at each other, each with a sensation of shock. Fiona was thinking that she had forgotten how devastatingly handsome Lord Peter was with his intense blue eyes and midnight-black hair and powerful, athletic body. Lord Peter was thinking that Fiona was a poor-looking dab of a girl and wondered why he had ever become so enraged, upset, and attracted by her.

She was no longer a threat to his peace of mind and so he smiled on her, and said, "Good evening, Miss Macleod. May I escort you upstairs?"

Fiona felt crushed. She had seen shock, followed by wariness, followed by amused relief in his eyes. She had meant to behave well and to practise on him the gentle arts of flirting and conversation as taught by the sisters. Some imp prompted her to say, "Are you sure you wish to be seen with me, my lord? I am even drearier than you remembered, is that not so? *I* did not choose this wretched gown."

Annoyed that she had guessed what he had been thinking, Lord Peter said crossly, "Either you are going to accept my escort or not, Miss Macleod. I do not want to stand in this draughty hall all evening."

He held out his arm.

Fiona put her hand on his arm. That slight physical contact sent a thrilling charge of emotion through Lord Peter's body. He led her up the stairs, looking down at her curiously, not knowing that Fiona was trying to stop herself from trembling, for she was suffering from the same violent physical reaction.

Lord Aubrey came up to them as they entered. "Havard," he cried. "Help yourself to food and drink and leave me to look after Miss Macleod."

"Evening, Aubrey," said Lord Peter. He disengaged himself with relief from Fiona and then immediately wanted to touch her again. He was annoyed at the admiration in Lord Aubrey's eyes and by the possessive way he crowded in on Fiona, monopolizing her and cutting her off from the rest of the company. Lord Peter took a glass of champagne and talked to some friends, all the while edging back in the direction of the door. He hated crushes like this and wondered why he had come. A Miss Dryden, doing her second Season, was eating him up with her eyes, and kept moving closer to him as she spoke, egged on by her doting mama. He backed away and then suddenly felt as if someone had applied one of the new galvanizing machines to his back. People were pressed against people all round the room because of the crush. But he knew, before he twisted about, that his back was pressed against Fiona's. He wondered what they would all think if he suddenly turned about and jerked her into his arms.

And then she moved away. He felt her move away. He heard Amy Tribble's loud voice making the farewells and Effy Tribble saying "Come along, Fiona," and Lord Aubrey begging permission to call.

He realised Mrs. Dryden had asked him a question and that she and her daughter were waiting for his answer. He said, "Yes," and then found to his horror that he had accepted an invitation to an al-fresco meal in the gardens of their Kensington villa.

He bowed and managed to get away. Surely such a strange and disturbing creature as Miss Macleod should be avoided at all costs. But perhaps he would just call on the morrow to reassure himself, to prove that his mind had been playing tricks, and to find she was every bit as ordinary as she had looked when he had seen her earlier in the hall.

Chapter 6

*Swans sing before they die—'twere no bad
thing
Should certain persons die before they sing.*
—Samuel Taylor Coleridge

LORD PETER HAVARD DIS-patched his servant with his card the following day. He had no intention of ever speaking to Fiona again. Hadn't he told her so when she had been so insolent to him in the Park? He should have cut her dead in Aubrey's hall. That physical excitement he had felt at her slightest touch was simply caused by anger and dislike.

He was sure Aubrey would call in person. He walked to his club to banish that picture of Lord Aubrey being entertained by Fiona.

The picture would not go away and was so annoying that it was with relief he saw his old friend, the Honourable Geoffrey Coudrey, known to one and all as Cully.

"I thought you were rusticating in the country," said Lord Peter, looking at his large, bearlike friend with affection. Cully was very hairy. He was the despair of his valet, who barbered him as often as his master would let him. Cully's thick thatch of nut-brown hair grew low on his forehead, and his chin always seemed to be dark blue. Lord Peter had seen him stripped for boxing and knew that Cully's chest was like a carriage rug.

"No, I'm weary of the country. Town's the place for me," said Cully. "Didn't work. Being the squire, I mean."

Cully had, the previous year, bought a fine property and land down in Kent. He had been disappointed in love and had convinced himself that society was all a sham and that he was more suited to a bucolic life.

"So what happens to the place now?" asked Lord Peter, sitting down opposite him.

"Oh, I'll sell it, of course. Land's in good heart and the old house is quaint and pretty if you can bear the Tudors, which I can't. Give me something modern every time."

Lord Peter, unlike his eldest brother the marquess, did not own any property of his own. He had made his money by shrewdly speculating in various business ventures. As the younger son of a duke he was free of responsibilities. He had a comfortable house in Town and during the winter he stayed in the country, either at his parents' home, or at the homes of his many friends. He had served in the army right up until Waterloo, a battle which had sickened him, as it had his commander, the Duke of Wellington. Like many of his class, he had still managed to attend the Season during various leaves, when he usually quickly found a suitable matron to dally with until it was time to go back to battle again.

"I'll buy it from you," said Lord Peter and then wondered how those words had managed to pop out of his mouth.

In fact, he looked every bit as surprised as Cully, who said, "Why? Someone turned *you* down?"

Lord Peter wanted to say he had been joking, he had not meant it, but the novel idea of having a home and land had quickened his pulses.

"No, I mean it," he said. "I've really done nothing much since I left the army but ruin my health. You know what it's like, Cully. Overheated drawing-rooms and boring misses on the one hand, and prize-fights on the other and silly races and trying to break one's neck."

"Lovely," said Cully, half closing his eyes. "Missed it all. Who's the lady?"

"There isn't one."

"Don't believe it. When a goer like you suddenly wants to put down roots, there's always a lady."

"Nonsense!" said Lord Peter, but he wondered whether Aubrey had marriage in mind.

Fiona was feeling very cross indeed with her chaperones. She could not understand why one of them was not present. Lord Aubrey was prosing on, and there were various other gentlemen in the drawing-room who had come to call. Fiona was bored with them all and felt that either Amy or Effy should have been there to speed them on their way.

But Amy had been asked to go riding with Mr. Haddon and was fearful of Effy coming too and so had said she would be back soon, only off for a quick trot. Effy had not wanted to confess to her meeting with Mr. Callaghan or even to say she had an appointment, lest the curious Amy demand to know where she was going. And so Fiona had been left alone.

But calls were only supposed to last a quarter of an hour, and one by one the gentlemen took their leave. Lord Aubrey seemed determined to stick it out. Fiona flashed an agonized look at Baxter, who went over and tapped the clock and said loudly, "I hope this isn't broken, miss. It seems as if my lord has been here almost half an hour, but since that cannot be the case, the clock must be running wrong."

This was too broad a hint for Lord Aubrey to ignore. He got reluctantly to his feet and begged Fiona to go driving with him the following afternoon. Fiona replied, truthfully, that she did not know what social arrangements her chaperones had made for her. Lord Aubrey bowed and said with meaning that he would be calling on the Misses Tribbles soon to ask them an important question. Fiona's heart sank, but then she remembered that she could tell the Tribbles the truth. It had never been possible to tell her aunt she just did not want to marry anyone, least of all any of the suitors who had come calling. It had been necessary to let them get as far as proposing and then frighten them off. If she had told her aunt that she had no intention of accepting any of the proposals she had seen looming on the horizon, then there had always been the danger that the Burgesses might have stepped in and arranged a marriage with the man's parents before Fiona had a chance to scare him off.

Her last caller gone, Fiona dismissed Baxter and went and looked moodily at her own reflection in the glass. Wide blue eyes stared back at her. Yvette had made her a pretty gown in blue tabinet and had dressed her hair in a becoming style. Now there was no one to see it, thought Fiona sadly, but she would not admit to herself that the "no one" was Lord Peter.

It would soon be five o' clock. Everyone who was any-one would be in the Park. No one made calls at five.

Fiona picked up a tambour-frame and sat down by the window and stuck the needle viciously into the cloth. Embroidery was not one of Fiona's accomplishments, a fact she had kept hidden from the sisters. The other day, Effy had asked her where her needlework was and Fiona had lied and said she had left her silks and frame in Tunbridge Wells. Effy had promptly bought her the nec-essary materials. Fiona was just wondering whether it would really be too low a trick to bribe Yvette to do some of it for her when Harris announced, "Lord Peter Ha-vard." The butler looked surprised to see that only Fiona was in the room, but he left the door open and hoped that would be enough to satisfy the conventions. A young unmarried lady must never, ever be alone in a room with a gentleman with the door shut.

Lord Peter advanced on Fiona. He did not know why he had come. Perhaps to reassure himself that she was as plain and uninteresting as he was determined she should be. But her eyes were blue, he realized with surprise, and her hair was really pretty.

"I am sorry to come so late," he said, "I have been buying a property."

"Where?" asked Fiona.

"In Kent. I have a mind to be a man of property."

"That I cannot imagine," said Fiona, sitting down and picking up the tambour-frame again.

"Why, pray?" asked Lord Peter, sitting in a chair beside her.

"I always imagine you wasting your time in ephemeral pursuits."

"What a very low opinion you have of me, to be sure."

His hair was very black and glossy, his face lightly tanned, his blue eyes deep and searching. He exuded an air of power and virility. Fiona's hand holding the needle trembled and she pricked her finger.

"I do not think you can sew, Miss Macleod," he said. "Most odd. All young ladies can sew."

"Not this one. I thought you were never going to speak to me again," said Fiona.

"I was very angry with you, and with reason." Her mouth was soft and pink and sweet. He stared at it, fascinated.

Fiona wished he would look away. She felt hot and prickly and she had a nasty pain in the pit of her belly. She looked up with relief as Harris entered bearing cakes and wine.

"Thank you," said Lord Peter. "We will serve ourselves."

Harris bowed and retreated. There was a sudden embarrassed silence. Lord Peter rose to his feet and poured two glasses of wine. Fiona breathed deeply and tried not to look at his legs.

Baxter came down the stairs and saw the drawing-room standing open. From the silence within, she supposed the room empty. The day was chilly and that open door was letting all the warmth from the drawing-room fire escape. She closed the door.

"You had better open it again," said Fiona, taking a glass of wine from Lord Peter.

"I don't bother about such silly conventions," he said, sitting down again. "You are quite safe with me."

How many women? thought Fiona, looking at his mouth. Forty? Fifty?

"Now what are you thinking?" he asked, amused.

"I was wondering how many women you have had," said Fiona.

"Miss Macleod!"

"Well, I did wonder," said Fiona huffily.

He turned in his chair and leaned towards her. "Does it matter to you, Miss Macleod?"

His eyes were warm and his voice caressing.

"You are flirting with me," accused Fiona. She set down her glass on a side table beside the discarded tambour-frame and glared at him.

"When you are angry, Miss Macleod," he said wonderingly, "your eyes turn silver. What colour would they turn, I wonder, were I to . . ."

"No!" said Fiona.

He set down his glass as well and leaned forward and took her chin in his hand. His knees were pressed against the side of her legs and she could feel her legs beginning to shake.

He stood up and put both arms on the arms of her chair and stooped over her. She stared up at his approaching mouth. His leaned closer and closer and his mouth found hers.

He was dimly reminded of the Peace Celebrations in Hyde Park—cannons firing, fireworks going off, noise and tumult and gladness. The war is over and I am come home. The only parts of their bodies that touched were their lips. His mouth sank deeper against hers and the room began to spin faster and faster until he was whirling off into a strange blackness, held to the earth by the feel of the warm young lips pressed so hard against his own.

He finally came to his senses and freed her mouth. She was shivering and he felt cold himself. "I am sorry," he whispered. "I don't know what came over me." He sat down again but took her hand in his and ran his thumb gently over the palm. "So what do we do about you and your odd views on marriage, Miss Macleod?"

"They are the same as your own, sir," whispered Fiona.

"And you are still of the same mind?"

Fiona stared at him with a drowned look. He frightened her. Her body frightened her. Should he turn cruel, he could hurt her more than any of Mrs. Burgess's lashings.

"I will never marry," she said.

"You little doxy," he said in a sudden fury. "I've a good mind to give you the shaking of your life."

He heard a step on the landing outside. He walked over to the fireplace and stood with his back to it. Fiona snatched up the tambour-frame. Amy strode in and looked at the pair curiously.

"Shouldn't be in here with the door closed. You know that, Lord Peter, even if she don't."

"It is of no matter," said Lord Peter. "I have overstayed my welcome."

He bowed and left.

Fiona forced herself to go on embroidering.

"Where is Effy?" demanded Amy.

"I do not know," said Fiona. "Out, I believe."

"Odd," said Amy. "I never would have gone and left you without a chaperone if I had known she meant to be absent."

"Baxter was with me for most of the afternoon. Lord Peter called unexpectedly."

"Well, I promised you we wouldn't interfere," said Amy, "but if he's what you want, you're going to have a hard time getting him. Nothing but a flirt. Don't take him seriously. Good Heavens, child! What crooked stitches! Is that the best you can do?"

"I'm afraid it is," said Fiona in a resigned voice.

"Never tell me that a Tartar such as Mrs. Burgess let you get away with stitches like that."

"I never got very far, you see. She would give me a piece

of plain hemming and then tut-tut when I couldn't get the stitches to lie neatly and would rip them out and set me to it again."

Amy shook her head in amazement. "And here we were thinking you didn't need any schooling. You had better start right away. Put that down. Yvette shall start you on a sampler."

"I *hate* sewing," said Fiona.

"What's that to do with it?" exclaimed Amy. "So do I. But the art of being a lady is having to do a whole lot of things you hate doing. All holes in your accomplishments must be plugged. I have a secret to tell you. I have been taking singing lessons. Now Effy does not know, nor Mr. Haddon. We are going to the Perrys' musicale tonight and I told Mrs. Perry of my new accomplishment and she said it would be a splendid idea if—when the diva has finished—I entertain the company with a short ballad."

"It sounds a very sedate sort of evening," said Fiona, thinking that Lord Peter would surely not attend and therefore she ought to feel comfortable. She remembered Lord Aubrey. "Oh, Miss Amy, Lord Aubrey will no doubt ask permission to pay his addresses. I do not want him."

Effy came in at that moment. She looked as if she had been lit up from within. Her eyes sparkled roguishly under quite the most dashing little hat Fiona had ever seen.

"Where have you been?" demanded Amy, and then added, "Never mind. Leave us, Fiona."

When Fiona left the room, Amy poured out the tale of Lord Peter's having been present, of how Fiona didn't want Aubrey, and of how she couldn't sew a stitch. Effy listened to the tirade with a dreamy half-smile on her face which made Amy break off and accuse Effy of having been at the gin again.

"No, no," said Effy with a secret smile. She made an obvious effort to bring her mind to present problems. "I think, Amy, that we had best appear not to be against Lord Peter, but we must contrive to keep them apart. It is a great pity about Aubrey. We shall not refuse him outright but tell him to wait a month or so, until the girl is more settled in London."

Mr. Haddon came that evening to escort the ladies to the musicale. Amy was amazed to notice that Effy hardly seemed aware of his presence.

There were not a great many people at the musicale. The Perrys were not very fashionable and lived in Chelsea, which Effy considered as being almost as bad as living in the country; she suspected the Perrys' neighbours of being shopkeepers and dreadful people like that. She voiced this thought aloud, and Fiona asked sharply what was so terribly disgraceful about respectable shopkeepers, whereupon Effy pressed the girl's hand and murmured, "So sorry, dear. I had for the moment forgot your unfortunate background."

"Then why attend the Perrys' if they are not bon ton?" asked Fiona.

"They are extremely endearing and likeable, and that's a novelty to society," said Amy. "And Brummell liked them, 'tis said."

Fiona was relieved to find only a small audience already seated in a small music room at the back of the house.

And then she twisted her head at the sound of a new arrival and saw Lord Peter Havard. She was all at once painfully aware that the chair on her left was empty. Would he sit next to her? An elderly gentleman made to sit down next to Fiona and she glared at him fiercely and dumped her reticule on the seat so that he backed away, muttering apologies.

94

Fiona twisted her head round again. He was still there, but he was chatting to a diminutive brunette and smiling down into her eyes. As yet unrealized jealousy and anguish mingled in Fiona's bosom and she removed her reticule from the empty seat and placed it on her lap and stared unseeingly in front of her.

Effy was sitting on Fiona's other side. "Where's Amy?" she whispered.

Fiona shook her head. She had forgotten about Amy's singing. Lord Peter was approaching. She could *feel* him coming nearer. He stopped at the end of the row. He bent to talk to an old woman. Of course she was terribly old, thought Fiona. Fifty if a day!

He straightened up. He saw the seat next to Fiona and his lips compressed into a firm line. He half turned away and then changed his mind and edged along the row of gilt chairs and sat down.

Both of them stared rigidly ahead.

The opera singer who was to entertain them came into the room. The pianist took his place. The audience settled back, prepared to be culturally bored and to enjoy it, for everyone knew that culture, like medicine, must be really nasty or it was not culture. But the soprano had recently been to Italy and had decided to entertain the company with popular Italian songs. She sang meltingly of love while Fiona's body seemed to melt into Lord Peter's side and she wondered how he had managed to move so close to her without shifting his chair. Fiona felt as if her soul and body were doing alternate somersaults.

It was a relief when the soprano finally finished.

Little Mrs. Perry held up her hands for silence. "Now, ladies and gentlemen," she cried, "I have a surprise for you. Our own diva—Miss Amy Tribble."

"Oh, no!" cried Effy weakly. "Someone stop her."

But Amy had bowed to the audience and was bowing to the pianist. Yvette had managed to persuade her to wear a new creation in scarlet merino. On her head, she wore a scarlet turban decorated with gold fringe. The style complimented her flat figure, and the long, trailing skirt of the gown hid her large feet. Her red hands were encased in white kid gloves. Fiona thought she looked very fine.

The pianist began to play and Amy opened her mouth and began to sing. It was a simple country ballad of a shepherd's love for his shepherdess, but Amy could not seem to hit the right key. The struggling pianist desperately tried to hit the same notes as Amy. Her voice was dreadfully flat. She cast anguished looks at the pianist as she battled to find the right note and the pianist threw anguished looks back.

Amy forgot the words and stood with her mouth wide open. Then, "Oh, slut on it!" she said cheerfully and went to read the words from the sheet of music on the piano, bending over the pianist, who cringed down on the stool. Someone at the back of the room let out a terrific snort of laughter. Fiona could feel laughter bubbling up inside her. Amy, having got over her initial stage fright, was now blissfully unaware of the horror of her performance or of the fact that her audience was slowly collapsing with mirth. She shrieked and roared while the pianist shut his eyes and ploughed manfully on.

When she had finished, there was a roar of applause. No one could remember having laughed so hard in ages. One man seized a bunch of flowers from a vase and ran to present them to Amy—Amy who had eyes only for Mr. Haddon and wondered why that gentleman was sitting with his arms crossed and staring at the tops of his shiny pumps.

"I shall tell her what a fool she made of herself," said Effy, fanning herself angrily.

"No, don't do that," said Mr. Haddon. "Too cruel. Only see how happy your sister is."

Lord Peter bent his head and whispered in Fiona's ear. "There is a garden here. Can you meet me there in ten minutes? I have something to say to you."

Then he moved away. Fiona wondered if he was going to propose marriage and whether she would have the courage to accept him. She thought of Lord Aubrey. Now, he would make an amiable and placid husband. No fireworks, no hurts, no jealousy or aching or burning.

Despite Mr. Haddon's protests, Effy tried to get through the press of people who were crowded about Amy to tell her forcibly that all were really laughing at her, but she could not get through. Then she thought of her wonderful afternoon with Mr. Callaghan, of how he had said he had never met anyone like her, of how he would like to spend the rest of his life with her, and she forgot all about everything and anything else. She was to meet him again on the Thursday, when the Dunsters had arranged a party on a barge on the Thames.

Mr. Haddon was worrying about what to do about Amy. He knew that cruel society would engage her for concert after concert, and when she finally found out everyone was laughing at her, the blow would be cruel indeed. But Amy, her face flushed and her eyes sparkling, was still accepting compliments. Mr. Haddon thought he had never seen her looking so happy or so well. He continued to worry about how to tell her she was making herself ridiculous.

So the three people who might have noticed Fiona's disappearance were all occupied with their own affairs.

Fiona slipped away to find the garden. There were windows leading to it from the music room, but that would have been too obvious. She found a sashed window in the library next door which overlooked the garden, pushed it up and looked out.

Lord Peter was walking up and down in the moonlight. "How did you get down?" called Fiona.

He came to stand under the window. "I simply walked out of the front door and around the side of the house."

"Why didn't I think of that," said Fiona.

"Never mind. Jump!"

"Jump?"

"It is only a small drop and I shall catch you."

Fiona drew back a little, suddenly afraid of him, afraid of the effect he had on her, afraid of his virility, and, more than anything, afraid of his experience. Just then a voice sounded outside the library door. Fiona climbed out onto the sill and dropped down into Lord Peter's arms.

"What do you want?" she whispered.

"I think I want you," he said in a low, husky voice. "Let me kiss you again."

He did not wait for her reply but folded his arms about her and kissed her very tenderly and softly on the lips, then harder, then harder still, until both were kissing furiously and straining against each other and muttering incoherent noises of passion. Her low-cut gown offered delicious moonlit areas of flesh to kiss. Fiona had to content herself with his face and mouth, as he was armoured in a dress coat and starched cravat.

He was just about to search down the neck of her dress with his questing hand when cold common sense told him he had to make up his mind and not go any further.

"Tell the Tribbles to expect my call tomorrow," he said.

"Do you think we should suit?" asked Fiona anxiously,

while inside her a warning voice screamed, "You must not marry. Marriage is pain and disaster."

"That is a risk I am prepared to take before you drive me mad, you Scottish witch." He cradled her face in his long fingers and looked searchingly down into her eyes, which were black, fathomless pools.

Amy was chattering away nineteen to the dozen. "I swear your voice has enchanted me!" cried a young man while turning slightly to wink at his friends. Amy blushed and turned her head away and then her mouth fell open, rather as it had done when she had forgotten the words of the song. For she had a sudden glimpse through the long windows of Lord Peter Havard and Fiona, clasped in each other's arms. Passion had made the couple careless and they did not realize they had moved under the music-room windows. Lord Peter glanced up and then pushed Fiona hurriedly into the shadows of the garden.

Amy started to sway like a poplar in a chopping wind. "Faint!" she gasped. "Air! Must have air!" Someone opened the French windows and Amy's admirers bore her down the steps into the garden.

Amy glared about her at the empty garden, silvered with moonlight. "I'm fine," she growled. "Champagne. Must have champagne."

What an original Miss Amy Tribble was! She was borne back indoors.

Lord Peter helped Fiona to her feet in the library after lifting her in through the window.

"Tomorrow," he whispered. He gave her one fierce kiss and then moved to the library door. "You go in first and I shall follow you later."

Fiona slid quietly out of the library. When she entered the music room, Effy caught hold of her. "What have you

99

been doing?" she snapped. "Come with me. Your hair is a mess and your mouth looks odd. All swollen and nasty."

During the journey home, Fiona said quietly, "Lord Peter Havard will call on you tomorrow."

"Why?" asked Amy bluntly.

"To ask your permission to pay his addresses to me."

Both sisters experienced a glow of sheer triumph. Lord Peter, that perpetual bachelor, had crumbled at last. What a prize! In the bliss of achievement, they quite forgot their disapproval of him.

Then both thought immediately of the Burgesses. They would be furious. The only thing to do was to get Fiona off to bed and plan a campaign.

Amy sat on the end of Effy's bed. "What should we do?" she asked. "By the look of Fiona this evening, it's perhaps better he should marry her and as soon as possible."

"What do you mean?"

"She had been well and truly kissed by that rat. Did you not mark her swollen lips and that bite on her neck?"

Effy turned scarlet. "Gentlemen do not go on thus except with tarts. We have not schooled Fiona well enough. Because she appeared so accomplished, we neglected to talk to her about the nastier side of romantic behaviour."

"I wouldn't call it *nasty*," said Amy. "I mean, if the man's spoony about her, stands to reason he gets carried away."

"You shock me," said Effy. "No gentleman ever behaves like that with the lady he plans to marry. No, Lord Peter Havard will not do. We shall see him and tell him that Fiona is too young and innocent to know her own mind. That he must wait. Then we shall tell her he didn't propose, he only apologized for his bad behaviour, and if that don't keep 'em apart, then nothing will. And talking of bad behaviour, there is something about your performance tonight, sister, that I should tell you. People were *laughing* at you, laughing fit to burst. I feel—"

"Jealous cat," said Amy with a grin. "I have indeed put your nose out of joint for once. I even left Mr. Haddon speechless." And before Effy could say another word, she left the room.

Chapter 7

I said to my heart between sleeping and
waking,
'Thou wild thing that always art leaping or
aching
For the black, or the fair, in what clime, in
what nation,
Hast thou not felt a fit of pitapat-ation?'
—*Charles Mordaunt, Earl of Peterborough*

FIONA WAS UP EARLY the next day, nervous with anticipation. She changed her dress several times and fussed with her hair, tried a little rouge and then wiped it off. She kept running to the window every time a carriage rattled over the cobbles outside.

By one in the afternoon, her rumbling stomach reminded her she had not eaten. She refused to go down to the morning room for breakfast but had it served on a tray in front of the window of her bedchamber. At last a carriage stopped outside. But the gentleman who descended was Lord Aubrey.

Fiona hoped the sisters would not forget their promise. But she half expected to be summoned to the drawing room to receive a proposal from the poet. It was with great relief that she saw Lord Aubrey leaving some ten minutes later. He did not look at all downcast. Fiona did not know the Tribbles had told him that there was every hope his suit might prosper if he was content to wait a little.

At two o'clock, she became weary of her long vigil, and was wondering whether to read a book or to go downstairs, where no doubt she would immediately be charged to start her sewing lessons, when she heard the sound once more of a carriage arriving in the street below.

She peered down from the window and breathed a sigh of relief as Lord Peter's tall, athletic figure bounded up the front steps.

Heart beating hard, she primped herself in the glass, and waited . . . and waited.

At last, she heard to her amazement Lord Peter's voice raised in farewell. Once more she went to the window. He was climbing into the carriage, his handsome face set in severe lines.

Fiona ran downstairs to the drawing-room. "Come in," said Effy when she saw the girl in the doorway.

"Why did you not send for me?" demanded Fiona. "It is customary, you know, after a gentleman has received permission to pay his addresses."

How irritating, thought the sisters, that the waif should suddenly be hell-bent on marriage after having refused so many—and marriage to such an unsuitable man. They had had a few moments' private discussion before Fiona appeared and had decided that Lord Peter must only be after the girl's money. Effy had put it about society that Fiona was rich. Everyone knew that younger sons of dukes did not have much in the way of the ready. Lord Peter was rumoured to be rich, but that was probably a hum. It was important that a girl who had been so hurt, so humiliated, and so disgusted by the very idea of marriage should not find herself locked up in a loveless one. They had told Lord Peter that he should wait and get to know Fiona better and that they could not possibly give him their permission yet. Seeing the fury on his face, Effy unwisely said that Fiona was in complete agreement.

She had said to Amy, after Lord Peter had left, that Fiona might return to her aunt if she found out they were lying, but Amy remarked that Lord Peter was in such a towering rage that his vanity would not allow him to approach the girl again.

"We did not send for you," said Effy, thinking rapidly how best to drive a wedge between the couple, "because Lord Peter did not propose. He came to apologize for his behaviour t'other night. Evidently he was too fast and too forward and feared he might have given you the wrong idea. He begs us to tell you that he was foxed."

Fiona agonizingly remembered the taste of his mouth. There had been no flavour of drink at all.

She feared marriage and yet she was deeply hurt. Had she planned to refuse him? She could hardly do that after allowing such intimate caresses. But none of the warring emotions in her mind showed on her face. She gave a little shrug. "Perhaps I might accept the poet after all," she said, and turned and went back upstairs.

"Now why have I got such a guilty conscience?" said Amy.

"I am sure we have done the right thing," said Effy firmly.

"It's all this worry about him being a rake," moaned Amy. "Is there any real proof?"

"Mrs. Vere-Cunningham says that he drove his carriage right into Hyde Park at the fashionable hour with no less than six demi reps screaming and ogling from it."

"When?"

"Ten years ago."

"The follies of youth," mourned Amy. "We may be making a mistake. I am sure Fiona was upset."

"Nothing to worry about," said Effy. "She took it very well."

It was truly amazing that both Lord Peter and Fiona managed to attend the Dunsters' barge outing on the river. Fiona had planned to manufacture a headache and stay at home and Lord Peter had not meant to go anyway. Each was furious with the other. But when Thursday morning arrived, both Fiona and Lord Peter became consumed with a desire to tell the other how miserable, double-dealing and disgraceful the other's behaviour had been.

Amy tried to persuade Mr. Haddon to call on Lord Peter and steal the invitation card from his mantelpiece, but Mr. Haddon replied firmly that in the first place he would not dream of doing such a thing, and in the second, Lord Peter had only to show his noble face to have himself admitted to the barge party, card or not.

Effy was not much help, thought Amy sourly. She was fluttering about in a day dream. Amy began to wonder if Effy had contracted a tendre for some secret and highly unsuitable lover. One of the servants? Harris? It was not impossible.

So Effy was the only happy member of the party that set out for the Thames. Lord and Lady Dunster's barge had been in the family since the days when state barges were more the thing. It was a long monster of a boat painted black and gold. A striped awning fluttered over the decks and an orchestra played and the guests wandered to and fro as if in a drawing-room rather than on a barge.

The first person Amy saw was Mr. Desmond Callaghan. "Look at that snake," she whispered. Then she looked down at her simpering and blushing sister in surprise and growing alarm. "You didn't, Effy," she exclaimed. "You couldn't."

"Mr. Callaghan apologized to me," said Effy fiercely. "If you interfere in this, Amy, *I shall never speak to you again!*"

"I am not going to allow it," said Amy, breathing heavily. She seized her parasol and raised it like a club.

"No, Miss Amy," said Mr. Haddon. "You will not make a scene. Your sister must make her own mistakes. Behave yourself!"

Amy looked at him with her mouth open. Then her eyes began to glow with a soft light. To Fiona's amazement, Amy said meekly, "Yes, Mr. Haddon."

"Good girl," he said, patting her shoulder. "Let me find you a glass of ratafia."

Despite her own worries, Fiona was tempted to giggle. There was something so funny about Amy's lamblike meekness.

And then the smile died on her lips. Lord Peter Havard had arrived, accompanied by a large, burly man with a low forehead. Cully had decided to go along with his friend on the outing.

She turned away and joined Amy and Mr. Haddon.

Lord Aubrey came up to Fiona and bent possessively

over her hand. Her heart sank. She knew Lord Aubrey would not leave her side for the whole of the party.

Having no desire to cross swords with *him,* she behaved in a dull, miserable way and barely said a word, not knowing that, since Lord Aubrey only wanted an audience, he felt more than ever she was the lady of his dreams.

When the barge moved off, Fiona wondered why it did not sink under the sheer weight of people. It was just like Lord Aubrey's party—a sad crush.

The day wore on, the lazy river chuckled under the boat, the sun shone down, and Fiona, trapped at Lord Aubrey's side, felt wretched. Occasionally the crowd parted to give her a glimpse of Lord Peter, who was always flirting with some lady or other. At last she felt she could not bear it any longer and said to Lord Aubrey, "I beg your pardon. I must look for Miss Effy." And before he could offer to accompany her, she had edged deftly away through the crowd.

But before she could get anywhere near Lord Peter, the barge slid into a mooring. The Dunsters were calling to their guests to go on shore. The shore turned out to be the lawns of a large riverside house. Long tables had been placed on the lawns, and, chattering with delight, the guests disembarked.

Fiona noticed there were little gilt cards with names on them in front of each place. There would be no chance of telling Lord Peter what she thought of him. Sponsored by the Tribbles she might be, but she was well below Lord Peter in rank. She found herself separated from the Tribbles as well. Her place was at one of the tables near the water on the sloping lawn, the more important in rank taking the tables near the house. It was small consolation to find that Lord Aubrey was seated far away from her as well.

Her companions were two middle-aged men; one on her right who concentrated on his food, and one on her left who spoke about hunting through the whole dreary meal.

The headache Fiona had been planning to pretend to have was now a reality. She breathed a sigh of relief when the long meal came to an end and the guests were urged to take a stroll in the gardens.

Effy walked off on Mr. Callaghan's arm. He was looking for a secluded spot in which to propose marriage, although he hoped somehow to get Effy's money and jewels without marriage. He felt sure, however, that if he proposed marriage, Effy would do anything he wanted. He led her away to an uncultivated part of the garden along by the river where there was a pleasant walk. To his delight, he saw a rustic bench by the shore and begged Effy to be seated.

"Before I say what is in my heart, Miss Effy," said Mr. Callaghan, "I must tell you the truth. I am a poor man. I have nothing to offer you but myself. I am ashamed. What it is to be poor!"

"I know," said Effy softly. "Amy and I found ourselves in the same predicament when Mrs. Cutworth died. We had been poor for so long and, well—it sounds so awful, so mercenary—but we could not help hoping she would leave us a fortune in her will. But she left everything to you, and that everything proved to be nothing but debts. Poor us. Poor Mr. Callaghan. Had it not been for Amy's idea to advertise ourselves as chaperones, we should have been in dire straits."

"Come, come," teased Mr. Callaghan, "you cannot tell me that being mere chaperones should bring about such a dramatic change in your fortunes."

Effy's mouth curved in a reminiscent smile. "Oh, it seemed like a magical happening. We were sponsoring Lady Baronsheath's daughter, Felicity. Lord Ravenswood, who married her, you know, befriended us from the first moment we met. We were anxious that Felicity, as our first 'job,' should not see how poorly we lived. Lord Baronsheath sent word to his servants in London to take up residence in Holles Place before Felicity's arrival and to decorate the house with the best pieces of his furniture and portraits of his ancestors. Then, when he married, not only did Lady Baronsheath give us a most generous bonus, but Lord Ravenswood gave us a present as well. I am so glad we have a new lady to sponsor, for what with the expense of managing a London house and servants, we were running out of money again. It is a precarious life and one which suits Amy very well, but I shall be so happy to settle down and never have to worry again." She looked at him shyly. "I always thought it would be hard to live in the country in genteel poverty, but with you, Mr. Callaghan, I could bear any hardship."

He looked at her, astounded. "But surely Mrs. Cutworth gave you money and jewels before she died!"

"Nothing," said Effy. "She did not really have any money to speak of, although, like you, we did not find that out until after she died." She shook her head sadly.

"Do you mean," said Mr. Callaghan in a thin voice, "that you are solely dependent on your work for an income?"

"But yes! Of course!" Effy wondered whether to tell him about the small annual amount she and Effy received from a family trust but decided it was too trifling a sum to mention.

The fact that the Tribbles had not tricked him out of anything belonging to Mrs. Cutworth should have restored Mr. Callaghan's faith in the human race in general and in the Tribble sisters in particular. But he felt cheated. He felt that Effy had led him on, had lied to him.

His highly painted face was covered in a thin sheen of sweat, and rouge began to stain the points of his shirt collar.

"But what is money to such as we?" said Effy gaily, rapping the sleeve of his coat with her fan.

"Money means a great deal," he said coldly.

"But lovers such as we have no need of such mundane things as money," cried Effy.

"Lovers? What *are* you talking about?" said Mr. Callaghan. "How could such as we be lovers—a young man and an old spinster?"

Effy shrank back on the bench as if she had been struck.

"Yes, *old* spinster," he repeated viciously. "Your wits must be wandering, ma'am. You have mistaken a young man's courtesy to an elderly lady. Good day to you!"

As he walked away, Effy began to cry.

Fiona wandered away from the chattering crowds. She did not want to see Lord Peter. She only wanted to be alone and find some shady spot in which to sit down.

Effy had moved away from the rustic bench into the trees to hide her grief and humiliation. Fiona sat down and drew patterns in the dust at her feet with the point of her parasol. She then drew Lord Peter Havard and sliced his head off. That made her feel better. The pain at her temples began to go away. The air was warm and a light breeze moved the young leaves of the trees above her head.

A shadow fell across her and she looked up. Lord Peter stood over her. The soft earth of the path had muffled his footsteps.

"What do you want?" asked Fiona.

"I want the luxury of telling you what I think of you,"

he said in a calm voice that belied his fury. "You allowed me to kiss you, so that you might have the pleasure of turning me down. Oh, I know the Misses Tribbles told me very pleasantly that you were not ready for marriage and they could not give their permission, but they are only rented chaperones and would never have stood in your way had you been willing!"

"I don't understand you," said Fiona, looking dazed. "They told me you had come merely to apologize for your bad behaviour and to say that you were foxed."

He stared at her blankly and then sat down beside her. "Do you want to marry me?" he asked.

Fiona felt a tumult of mixed emotions—elation, excitement, relief, and fear. She was afraid of marriage. She dreaded finding herself locked in a marriage full of rows and scenes and bitter recriminations. What if he regretted marrying the daughter of a tradesman? But his eyes were so very blue and steady and serious. She took a deep breath. "Yes," she said.

"Then I shall not speak to the Tribbles again. I shall speak to your aunt and uncle."

"Alas, they will not give their permission. They were anxious that the Tribbles find me someone outside the aristocracy."

"I can be very persuasive," he said. "I shall reverse the normal procedure—a proper proposal to you first and permission from your aunt and uncle afterwards. Do not tell the Tribbles about this. For some mad reason of theirs, they do not consider me suitable either."

He took a handkerchief out of his pocket and put it on the ground and then knelt on one knee in front of her.

Amy was supremely happy. Although Mr. Haddon had gone off to speak to some friends, she was content to sit in the sunshine and enjoy the soporific effects of too much food and wine. The Dunsters had asked her to sing to the guests on the barge going home. She smiled to herself as she anticipated the sound of the applause. She had even stopped worrying about Effy. Her sister's friendship with Mr. Callaghan would normally have infuriated Amy, but her new-found success made everything else seem of little significance—except Mr. Haddon, of course, and he would admire her the more, the more in demand she became. Mr. Haddon had not found the courage to tell Amy she was making a fool of herself.

Amy was sitting in the sun with her back to the long French windows of the drawing-room. From inside came the chatter of the guests who had gone to tour the house and to look at Lord Dunster's collection of miniatures.

And then Amy heard Lady Dunster's voice very clearly. Lord Dunster was slightly deaf, and so Lady Dunster always spoke in a very loud and carrying voice. "I have a treat for all of you when we set sail again," boomed Lady Dunster. "I have asked Miss Amy Tribble to entertain the guests."

This was greeted with loud cheers and laughter. Although the guests inside were unaware that Amy was outside listening, she smiled modestly and looked down.

Then a woman said, "Miss Amy is an Original. I declare I never laughed so hard in my life as when I heard her sing the other night."

The listening Amy stiffened and frowned. But there was worse to come. A man's voice said, "Isn't she marvellous? She sings like a crow with a sore throat, and that poor piano player was fighting his way up and down the keys trying to find a note to match that horrible voice."

Another man said, "I do not think there is one note in

the music scale, either Chinese or English, that Miss Amy Tribble could hit. My dear Lady Dunster, how are we to keep our faces straight? How are we to stop dying of laughter?"

With dreadful clarity, Lady Dunster said, "But, my dears! When Miss Amy sings, she is quite oblivious to anything and everything. Laugh as much as you like!"

Amy got up slowly. She felt very old and stiff. She moved across the lawns as if on stilts. A few people hailed her, but she stared at them blindly. She blundered off into the uncultivated bit of the garden, bumping into trees and bushes, desperate to put as much distance as possible between herself and those ugly, mocking voices.

Hot tears began to course down her cheeks. She had never felt quite so old, homely, and unloved. Perhaps Mr. Haddon had been secretly laughing at her as well.

She bumped into the weeping figure of her sister, Effy. Amy stopped short and scrubbed her eyes with her glove.

"What's the matter?" demanded Amy harshly.

"It . . . it's Mr. Callaghan," sobbed Effy.

Amy's humiliation was temporarily forgotten. "That snake!" she cried. "Where is he? What has he done?"

"He's gone," said Effy in a small voice. "I've been wicked, Amy . . . an old fool. He courted me because he thought I had money, just the same way as he made a fool out of Auntie."

Amy put her arms round her sister and hugged her close. "Don't cry, Effy," she said. "I am as foolish as you. I . . . oh, Lor'!"

She broke off in consternation. As she hugged Effy's slight figure, she had been looking over her shoulder. There at the water's edge was a pretty tableau. Lord Peter

Havard was just getting down on one knee in front of Fiona Macleod.

"We must stop them!" cried Amy. She swung Effy around and pointed.

"Oh, dear," said Effy. Both sisters thought the same thing at once. The Burgesses would be furious. The Burgesses would say they had failed. With amazing speed and agility, Effy sped straight for the River Thames and along the fallen trunk of a tree that overhung the water. Holding her nose firmly, she jumped in, a thing she would normally never have dreamt of doing but she had been shaken out of her wits by Mr. Callaghan.

"Help!" screamed Effy. "I can't swim."

Breathless with admiration for her sister's quick-wittedness, Amy ran to the water's edge. "Save her. Save my sister," she called to Lord Peter.

Lord Peter sighed. "Excuse me, my love," he said to Fiona.

He marched into the river. The water did not even cover the top of his Hessian boots. He reached forward and picked up the sodden bundle that was Effy Tribble by the scruff of her neck, lifting her clean out of the deeper part of the river and dumping her on the bank.

"How good of you to save her," said Amy.

Effy sat up, shivering.

"Can you tell me why Miss Effy should decide to throw herself in the river?" said Lord Peter, eyeing both sisters cynically.

"Yes, why?" came Mr. Haddon's voice as the nabob hurried towards the group.

Amy looked wildly at Effy and Effy stared in consternation at Amy. If Lord Peter had not yet had a chance to propose, then there was still hope. Effy thought of the terrible Mr. Callaghan.

"I wanted to end it all," she said. "Mr. Callaghan insulted me."

"How? Why?" asked Fiona.

"He led me on," said Effy miserably., "and then spurned me most cruelly."

"I shall attend to him," said Mr. Haddon grimly. "Get Miss Effy back to the house. She must find dry clothes."

The little group hurried Effy back along the woodland path and across the lawns. They were almost at the house when Mr. Haddon saw Mr. Callaghan.

Mr. Haddon drew off one of his lavendar kidskin gloves and advanced on Mr. Callaghan.

Guests stared in amazement as Mr. Haddon struck Mr. Callaghan full across the face with his glove. "You have offended a friend of mine," said Mr. Haddon. "Name your second, sir!"

Mr. Callaghan looked wildly round for escape. But duelling, although outlawed, was considered prime sport. To the Fribble's dismay, a languid dandy called Jeremy Bessamy promptly offered to second him. Lord Peter in an amused voice offered to second Mr. Haddon.

As Effy vanished inside the house, Mr. Callaghan found it had all been arranged with frightened rapidity—pistols at eight o'clock in the morning at Chalk Farm in two days' time.

It was a dismal sail home for Amy. She refused with dignity to sing a note. She was furious with Effy, Effy who sat in borrowed clothes, sipping champagne and chatting and laughing. For two men were to fight a duel over Effy. Amy could have killed her sister. What if Mr. Callaghan killed Mr. Haddon?

She had asked Lord Peter to try to get Mr. Haddon to change his mind, having failed to do so herself, but Lord Peter had only smiled at her and said that if she stopped

116

interfering in his romance with Fiona, then he would think about it.

As for Mr. Callaghan, he sat as far away as possible from the Tribbles and Mr. Haddon. He had tried to talk himself into bravery by reminding himself that Mr. Haddon was an old man. But Mr. Haddon looked remarkably spry, and there had been a deadly gleam in his steady grey eyes when he had issued that challenge. By the time the barge reached London, Mr. Callaghan had decided to escape to the Continent.

Frank was slouched by the fireplace, moodily picking his teeth, when his master charged into the room, followed by his valet.

"Where's the fire?" asked Frank, getting to his feet.

"Make yourself useful, fellow," snapped Mr. Callaghan. "I am going abroad."

Frank's eyes lit up. "I must say as how I've always wanted to see foreign parts," he said.

"You're not coming, you lummox," said Mr. Callaghan. "I'm only taking John." John was his valet and general servant. "You'll find two imperials on top of the wardrobe in the bedroom. Start packing the necessary while John and I go round to the livery stables to rent a travelling carriage."

"What am I to live on while you're away?" asked Frank, aghast.

"I've credit with the Three Jolly Chairmen round the corner," said Mr. Callaghan. Frank tried to protest. The last time he had been to that coffee-house with an order for Mr. Callaghan, they had told him in no uncertain terms that there would be no further credit until Mr. Callaghan settled his bill.

When master and valet had gone, Frank sank slowly

back into the chair. Why had he ever listened to this fop with his rubbish about the equality of men and his Robin Hood ideas of taking from the rich and giving to the poor?

Frank felt so angry he thought he would burst. He knew now that Mr. Callaghan did not believe a word of his preaching and had been out only to make mischief.

Mr. Callaghan needed to be taught a sharp lesson.

Feeling a bit shaky at the enormity of what he was about to do, Frank went into the bedroom and took down the two cases from the top of the wardrobe and then started to fill them with the precious objets d'art that were lying around and all the items of Mr. Callaghan's clothing he had coveted.

He literally struck gold at the back of a drawer of cravats—two rouleaux of guineas.

He thought about Bertha, the chambermaid. It would be fun to have a companion on the road—for Frank knew he must get out of London as quickly as possible.

But to see Bertha would mean hanging about Holles Street. He decided to make his own escape and return to find Bertha when he was sure Mr. Callaghan had left London.

Frank was well on his way to the City to catch any stage anywhere that had a free seat when Mr. Callaghan returned to find his apartment looking as if a bomb had hit it. Drawers were hanging open or upended on the floor, and, worst of all, his best pair of Hessian boots—two sizes too small for Frank—had been stuffed into the red-hot ashes of the sitting-room fireplace.

"Get the Runners! Get the militia!" screeched the valet.

But Mr. Callaghan could think only of a field at Chalk Farm and of Mr. Haddon's stern eyes measuring him up from behind the long barrel of a duelling pistol. He still had money hidden under the floor-boards, for he never paid any tradesmen unless absolutely forced to. He almost wept with relief to find it still there. Frank could go free. All Mr. Callaghan wanted to do was to put as many miles as possible between himself and Mr. Haddon.

Chapter 8

It is an infallible law of nature that those who injure, either hate or despise the object. Hence the contempt and acrimony with which men speak of women.

—The Lady's Magazine, *May 1810*

AMY TRIBBLE'S JEALOUSY OF her sister took second place to her frantic worry for the safety of Mr. Haddon.

She was tempted to alert the authorities to stop the duel, but was afraid of Mr. Haddon's finding out she had done so. She knew, in those circumstances, it was highly possible he would never speak to her again.

It was Effy who all unwittingly gave her a splendid idea. Effy had decided that Fiona needed sharp and fast education in men. She instructed Amy to dress as a man in order to illustrate Effy's talks to Fiona and show her that the most charming men were often rakes, the sort of men who promised marriage only to get their own evil ends *without* marriage.

Amy was half-heartedly entering into this charade the day before the duel when a marvellous idea came to her. She would dress up as a Bow Street Runner, travel out to Chalk Farm, and stop the duel. That Mr. Haddon would recognize her never crossed her mind. Amy was a romantic, and the books she liked to read often portrayed heroines dressing up as men and they were never recognized by the hero. Having come to this decision, she brought her mind back to the present and threw herself into her role of dashing rake with such conviction that Fiona began to feel uneasy and wonder if Lord Peter really meant to marry her. He had promised to travel to Tunbridge Wells directly after the duel, but he had not called, and his absence was bringing back all her fears of marriage.

Ladies often dressed up as men to attend masquerades, and so it was not considered odd by the shopkeepers to attend to a lady who was anxious to buy a red waistcoat to fit herself. She at last met with success at a tailor's who had made such a waistcoat for a customer who had not turned up to collect it. It was a trifle large, but Amy was tired of searching.

Amy hardly slept that night. She was anxious to leave as early as possible in the morning. Now that she had made up her mind to aid Mr. Haddon, she felt no nervousness as she set out atop a tall, raw-boned mare to Chalk Farm. Amy prided herself on having "bottom."

Bottom was one of the most prized virtues in the Regency. It meant having coolness, courage, and solidity. It was a necessary quality in this age where epidemics such as typhoid, cholera, or smallpox could wipe out whole families. Even the most effete fop learned at an early age to endure pain, as flogging was so prevalent in public schools that there were several rebellions, one in Harrow lasting over three weeks. The strange thing about the men of the Regency was that their pistolling, boxing, flogging, gaming, boozing, and enduring were combined with sensitivity. They were not bruisers, cried easily, had a real enjoyment of literature, wit, culture, delicacy, and eccentricity. Although bottom was a masculine virtue, women such as Amy who longed to have the freedom men enjoyed, often secretly considered themselves to be every bit as strong and resilient as men, and often they were.

Once Amy reached Chalk Farm, she nudged her mare off the road and made her way to the duelling ground by a circuitous route through the trees.

It was a beautiful morning. The sun was already spreading warmth over the surrounding countryside, and wreaths of mist were rising from the fields and circling round the boles of the trees. Amy dismounted and hid behind a tree. By peering around it, she had a clear view of the grassy field where the duel was to take place.

She had decided that since she could not arrest the antagonists, being hardly able to march them off to the round-house, she would need to charge them and bluster and lecture and then pretend to let them off, provided the duel did not go ahead.

Soon she began to feel hot and uncomfortable. She was wearing false side-whiskers and her face itched. She had stuffed a pillow under her waistcoat to give herself the portly appearance she considered necessary for the masquerade.

Then she heard the rattle of carriage wheels and creaking of joists. Mr. Haddon arrived, then a surgeon, then Lord Peter Havard, and then Mr. Jeremy Bessamy. They all stood for a moment in a group talking and examining a box of duelling pistols.

Mr. Haddon was wearing a black coat buttoned up to the neck, black knee breeches, and top boots. His hair under his tall beaver hat was tied at the nape of his neck with a black ribbon.

The men and Amy waited and waited. Suddenly Mr. Bessamy cried, "Here he comes!" Mr. Bessamy was mistaken. It was only a carriage passing along the road beyond the field, but Amy did not know that.

She leaped from behind her tree. "Hold hard!" she cried in a gruff voice. "I arrest all of you in the King's name!"

The pillow under her waistcoat proved too much of a strain for the buttons, which started to pop, and she was waving a large pistol which she had bought for the occasion but did not know had a hair-trigger. It went off with a loud report and put a ball clean through Mr. Bessamy's hat. Mr. Bessamy uttered a faint bleating sound and swooned.

Lord Peter rushed to Mr. Bessamy and knelt down and then swung round in a fury to face Amy. But the Bow Street Runner was being led away through the trees by Mr. Haddon.

"Help me. I am seriously killed," cried Mr. Bessamy, recovering and clutching hard at Lord Peter's lapels and nearly toppling him over.

"I suggest you stay here in hiding, Miss Amy," Mr. Haddon was saying severely, "and I shall go back and tell them that because of your dangerous behaviour you have decided not to report the matter."

"Who's Miss Amy?" demanded Amy in a shaky voice.

"You silly goose," said Mr. Haddon. "Do as you are told."

Amy waited and waited, feeling ridiculous and dreading Mr. Haddon's wrath. She heard the sound of carriages driving off. Amy trembled, hoping Mr. Haddon had left as well. But he eventually reappeared and stood looking at her. "Now, Miss Amy," he began severely. But his eyes crinkled up with laughter, and he put a handkerchief over his face. It was to no avail. He laughed and laughed as he had not done since his boyhood, while Amy shuffled her large feet and felt ready to die of embarrassment.

"You ridiculous girl," said Mr. Haddon, recovering at last, and Amy began to feel a little glow of pleasure despite her distress. It was wonderful to be called a girl. "You cannot return to Holles Street in those clothes," said Mr. Haddon. "I assume you said nothing to Miss Effy?"

Amy dumbly shook her head.

"Then we shall go to some posting house for breakfast and I will try to find you a ready-made gown and bonnet. You are very brave and I thank you, Miss Amy. But there was no need for such heroics. Mr. Callaghan appears to have no intention of showing up."

"How did you recognize me?" asked Amy.

But Mr. Haddon only began laughing again, so hard that he could not reply.

Lord Peter arrived at last in Tunbridge Wells two days later, put up at the best inn, and sent his card around to the Burgesses.

He decided that once he had secured their permission, he would return to Town and tell Fiona the news and then travel to that property in Kent and see if it was as good a place as Cully had described.

A brief note arrived back from the Burgesses, inviting him to dinner. He sighed with relief. Things looked promising. Provided he behaved in as sober a manner as possible, he felt sure he could persuade them to give him their permission to marry Fiona.

Lord Peter was well aware of the rules laid down for gentlemen dining out. An etiquette book stated that the Diner Out "must keep the character of a good-natured fellow. It must be his study to display a certain good-natured dullness." Intellect was something one was expected to have but not to display, especially in the company of ladies.

He dressed in his best and made his way to the Burgesses at five o'clock, Mr. and Mrs. Burgess considering the new later hours of dining but one step removed from decadence.

They lived in a large mansion full of cold, dark rooms. Mrs. Burgess had a hatred of dust, and although she would never stoop to do such a menial task as dusting, she never had fires lit after the first of March, whether it was blowing a blizzard outside or not. Fires created dust.

The gardens were dull. Bright flowers were considered immoral, and so the depressing laurel bushes and yew hedges and the marble rocks bordering the lawns gave the gardens all the cheer of a well-kept cemetery.

After the formalities of greeting had been exchanged, Mr. Burgess said, "We have invited you here, Lord Peter, for we fear you may wish to ask for Fiona's hand in marriage. Such a marriage would not be suitable. The aristocracy should never marry out of their class."

"Just what I am always saying myself," said Lord Peter with a look of amiable stupidity.

"Then why are you come?" asked Mrs. Burgess in surprise.

"I do not believe in girls' marrying for money," said Lord Peter, "and I wish your assurances as to Miss Macleod's character. I am a very wealthy man."

"But Fiona is an heiress!" exclaimed Miss Macleod.

"Dash me," said Lord Peter with a vacuous laugh. "I wondered why it was she appeared to attract every fortune-hunter in London."

"Good gracious," exclaimed Mrs. Burgess. Then she relaxed. "I am sure the Misses Tribble would not allow our niece to marry anyone like that."

"Still," said Lord Peter, "the fact remains that Miss Macleod does not seem to like the idea of marriage, and rumour has it she has had several proposals and turned them all down." Lord Peter was guessing, but it was a safe guess. In these inflationary days of the Regency, any heiress received a great many proposals.

Mr. and Mrs. Burgess exchanged glances. They did not want to confess to Lord Peter that they were not quite sure whether Fiona had actually ever received proposals of marriage or had strangely managed to give her suitors a violent disgust of her before they got to the point.

Mr. Burgess found his voice. "I must confess, Lord Peter, our disapproval of you was based on our first meeting. You were in a curricle race on the London Road."

"Egad, what you must think!" said Lord Peter. "I did not want to betray my friend and tell you the truth. I was trying to catch him to give him a horsewhipping. He had been rude and ungracious to an elderly couple at an inn at which we had stopped for refreshment—a vicar and his wife. I did not realize until then that my friend had such a hatred of the clergy. You must understand my horror. He had to be taught a lesson."

"Quite so, quite so," said Mr. Burgess, thawing visibly. "But why did you lie to us?"

"You did not know me; my quarrel was with my friend, and I did not want to betray his bad behaviour to anyone else. Do forgive me."

"Yes, yes," said Mrs. Burgess. "Your behavior does you credit."

Dinner was announced.

Lord Peter was amazed at the paucity of the fare. He would not have allowed such meager helpings to be served in his own servants' hall. There was a thin, watery soup, two tiny slivers of plaice followed by boiled mutton and overcooked vegetables, and rather dusty-looking tartlets, all washed down by a canary wine so peculiar in taste that Lord Peter wondered if some vintner had assumed in a mad moment that canary was made from a distillation of those birds rather than hailing from the vineyards of the Canary Islands.

Lord Peter discoursed with amazing stupidity on several topics of the day. Transportation, he said, was too good for criminals and a waste of public money; mass hangings such as they had had at Tyburn in the golden days of the last century ought to be reintroduced. The Burgesses nodded and smiled and ate with a hearty appetite. The Whigs, drawled Lord Peter, were all Jacobites at heart, and had lost his respect when they had supported the American colonists. So amazed and approving were Mr. and Mrs. Burgess at this piece of wisdom that they failed to observe that Lord Peter had not yet been born at the time of the colonial wars. Slavery, said Lord Peter expansively, was good for trade, and he had no sympathy with the abolitionists. By the end of the dreadful meal, Mr. and Mrs. Burgess had begun to think this paragon almost too good for their niece. With a gracious smile and a silent nod of approval to her husband, Mrs. Burgess retired to leave the gentlemen to savour quite the worst port Lord Peter had ever allowed to pass his lips.

"I must confess we were sadly mistaken in you," said Mr. Burgess. "I know my wife will now join me in giving our permission to this marriage. But a word of warning. Fiona can be wayward. I have always found the application of the birch rod necessary."

Lord Peter clutched his glass and with a heroic effort refrained from throwing its contents in Mr. Burgess's face. He reflected that had they not given him permission to marry Fiona, he would have taken her straight to Gretna Green to marry her immediately and save her from ever having to return to monsters such as these.

So enchanted were Mr. and Mrs. Burgess with him that he found some difficulty in taking his leave. It was only nine o'clock when he returned to the inn and yet he felt he had been locked up in that villa for years.

He was passing through the entrance hall of the inn when he was hailed by Captain Freddy Beaumont. "Going back to my regiment," said the captain cheerfully. "Care to share a bottle of port with me?"

"Gladly," said Lord Peter. Captain Freddy had seemed charmed by Fiona at the ball Lord Peter's parents had given, but had shortly afterwards left Town. Lord Peter reminded himself that now he had nothing to fear from any competition.

How jolly it was to have sane company and a decent bottle of port, thought Lord Peter, stretching his long legs under the taproom table.

It was only after two glasses had been drunk and the captain was roaring for more that Lord Peter realized Freddy Beaumont was quite drunk.

"Are you celebrating something?" asked Lord Peter.

"On the road back from m'parents," said the captain. "Gawd. Awful business, parents. Treat me like a toad and then charge me with lack of affection. Eugh!"

"I haven't been seeing my parents," said Lord Peter, "but I think I feel the same as you. As a matter of fact, I was here getting permission to pay my addresses to a certain lady."

"Getting married?" asked the captain. *"You?"*

"Yes, I," said Lord Peter. "To Miss Fiona Macleod."

"Demme, put it there!" said the captain, stretching out his hand, seizing Lord Peter's and wringing it fervently. "What a lady. Hey, waiter! Another bottle. Stap me, if you ain't the bestest Trojan ever, Havard. Better'n me any day."

"I am glad my choice meets with your approval," said Lord Peter, raising his eyebrows.

"The modern age of liberty is here," cried the captain. "Your health, b'Gad! Wanted her for m'self. But too old-fashioned and frightened of the parents, don't you see."

Lord Peter stared at him in surprise.

"Yes, when Miss Macleod told me, I was struck all of a heap," went on the captain. "Yet why should we rakes turn up our noses because a lady falls once from grace? You're a hero, Havard."

Lord Peter was about to ask Captain Freddy what the deuce he meant, but he suddenly had a shrewd idea that if the captain knew he had not the faintest idea what he was talking about, then the captain would keep silent.

"Well, it was a bit of a shock, I agree," said Lord Peter. "But I'm hardly a saint myself."

"Exactly!" said the now very drunk captain, thumping the table energetically. "Mind you, would have been easier to take had it been a gentleman and not some servant."

Lord Peter relaxed. Charles, the footman. Fiona must have told the captain that lie about being in love with a footman.

"You could have knocked me all of a heap," went on the captain, "when I proposed marriage and she looked at me in that sweet way of hers and said she was not a virgin."

Lord Peter felt himself grow cold.

"These girlish follies must be forgiven," he said with a lightness he did not feel. "But I trust you will not breathe a word of this to anyone. I would not like to have to call you out."

"On my oath," said the captain, "if you had not obviously already known her dark secret, I would not have said a thing."

Lord Peter changed the subject and finally took his leave and went up to his bedchamber. He sat by the open window with his head in his hands and thought hard. Could Fiona have been lying? But she had kissed him with a fierceness and passion not common in ladies, and certainly not in unmarried ones. But what right had he to demand a virgin in his marriage bed when he himself had lost his virginity such a long time ago and had bedded so many?

And yet the intellect could cry one thing and the emotions would not listen. He was fiercely jealous of this footman, shocked and disgusted at Fiona's behavior, but he knew he could never give her up.

Morning brought sunshine and sanity. He could not believe it of Fiona. All he had to do was to ask her.

When he reached London, he went directly to Holles Street. The Tribbles were both at home and agreed with great reluctance to receive him.

He told them of his visit to the Burgesses and of how he had secured their permission. All would have gone well from there had it not been for Effy's vanity. She felt piqued that this lord had gone over their heads, so to speak. People might say that it was Mr. and Mrs. Burgess themselves who had secured this splendid match. On top of that, her humiliation at the hands of Mr. Desmond Callaghan still rankled. Men were cheats and deceivers and not to be trusted.

"You cannot expect us to welcome your suit," said Effy huffily. "Fiona is too young for you. Let me speak plain, you are a man of . . . er . . . great experience and much older than she."

Lord Peter did not notice that Fiona had arrived and was standing in the doorway.

"May I point out, madam," he said icily, "that under the circumstances you should be down on your knees

131

begging me, begging anyone, to take the girl off your hands."

All the way back to London, Lord Peter had told himself that Fiona had lied to the captain. But unreasoning jealousy had raised its ugly head. Also, he was used to getting his own way and felt he had suffered enough interference from these spinsters.

"What do you mean?" demanded Amy.

"Simply that I have reason to believe your charge is not a virgin!"

Fiona came into the room. Lord Peter rose, his face red. He faced Fiona defiantly. "You told a certain gentleman of my acquaintance that you had lost your virginity to a footman. Is that the case?"

Fiona bowed her head in shame. How could she confess to that dreadful lie? Her lies about madness and consumption could be forgiven, but no lady ever lied about her virginity.

She opened her mouth to speak, her eyes wide with distress and shining with tears. Lord Peter took her distress for guilt and his heart was wrenched.

"What a brute I am," he said softly, taking her hands in a warm clasp. "It makes no difference, my love, and I have secured your aunt and uncle's approval."

Both Amy and Effy gazed at Fiona in horror. They too misread her shame as being the shame of guilt.

Amy cleared her throat and said in a small, tired voice, "I really think, under the circumstances, you should accept him and be grateful, dear. None of us will ever speak of this matter again."

This is dreadful, thought Fiona. I must see him alone and confess when he is in a softer mood.

Lord Peter turned to the Tribbles. "I am purchasing a property in Kent. I shall obtain a special licence before I leave Town so that Fiona and I may wed on my return. With your permission, I think a simple ceremony here would be in better taste rather than in church."

The Tribbles sorrowfully bowed their heads. They had failed. No glorious society wedding to broadcast their success. But both had become very fond of Fiona and kept silent.

When Lord Peter had left, Fiona sank down in a chair and looked at them sadly. "I have a confession to make," she said.

"Please don't," said Effy, putting up her hand. "There are some things we would rather not hear."

"But don't you see," cried Fiona wretchedly. "I lied to Captain Freddy Beaumont as I lied to the others; only in his case, the lie was dreadful. I said I had been seduced by a footman and that is untrue!"

"Are you telling the truth for once?" demanded Amy.

"Yes," said Fiona. "Oh, yes."

"Oh, Lor," said Amy. "Now he thinks he's doing a noble thing by marrying a tart. I had better send a message round to his house."

"Oh, please let me wait until he returns and talk to him," said Fiona. "Right at this moment I feel he would be more furious to find I had lied than relieved to find I was still a virgin. He might cry off."

"Well," pointed out Amy brutally, "that might be no bad thing. He is not at all suitable. Rakes don't change."

"You dreadful girl," sobbed Effy. "We must have a society wedding. You cannot be married in this hole-and-corner fashion. I could *shake* you!"

"It all comes from not being able to make up your stupid mind," howled Amy, losing her temper. "Lie after lie after damned lie. You don't want to get married and then you turn about and demand a man who will break your heart. Did you never think of us when you were playing your idiotic tricks? I don't want to see any more of you just now. Go away before I strike you!"

Fiona trailed from the room. She felt small and ridiculous and grimy. She almost wished the sisters had beaten her as Mr. Burgess used to beat her. They had shown her many kindnesses, and this was how she repaid them. Lord Peter must be persuaded of the truth and if he was so furious with her that he cried off, then it was no less than she deserved.

She put on her cloak and bonnet and made her way downstairs. She did not know where Lord Peter lived, but somehow she would find out and hope she would be in time to speak to him before he left.

She slipped from the house and nearly bumped into Bertha, the chambermaid, who was carrying a large basket and looking frightened and guilty. Normally, Fiona would have asked the girl where she was going. Servants carrying large baskets and dressed for a journey were either taking their annual leave or had been dismissed. But she did not want to stop even for a moment. She squared her shoulders and set out for Berkeley Square to confront Lord Peter's parents.

Chapter 9

Love is a circle that doth restless move
In the same sweet eternity of love.
—Robert Herrick

I T IS HIGHLY DOUBTFUL if the Duke or Duchess of Penshire would have received so undistinguished a person as Miss Fiona Macleod had their son not sent them a curt message saying he was about to announce his engagement to her.

Fiona had no intention of seeing either of them. She hoped to get Lord Peter's address from the Penshire's butler.

But when she timidly presented her card and her request to the butler, he merely placed the card on a silver salver and made his way upstairs, telling her to wait.

The Duke and Duchess were entertaining various society members in their saloon and gleaning as much as possible about this Miss Macleod when the butler entered. They had just learned to their horror from a Scottish earl that Fiona's father had been in trade. Both concealed their dismay as well as they concealed their surprise when the duchess first read Fiona's name on her card and then passed it to her husband.

Their eyes exchanged an unspoken message and the duke rose to his feet. "Tell this young person," he said in a low voice to the butler, "that I shall be with her directly. Put her in the library."

The butler bowed and withdrew. Fiona longed to flee. She said all she wanted was Lord Peter Havard's address, but the butler, like his master, had learned the gentle art of falling deaf when it suited him at an early age and merely held open the door of the library and ushered her in.

Had Fiona guessed that Lord Peter's parents had already been told of his intention to marry her, she would have fled. She decided as she waited to tell whoever came to see her—the duke's secretary?—that Lord Peter had lent her a book of poems and she wished to return them.

Then the door of the library opened and the duke walked in. He had seemed a round, jolly sort of man when Fiona had first seen him at the ball. Now, he appeared formidable. Although corpulent, he was as tall as his son, and his eyes were just as blue and piercing.

He made Fiona an elegant bow and then begged her to be seated.

He looked at her in silence, waiting for her to speak.

"And it please you, your grace," began Fiona, but the words came out in a sort of croak. She cleared her throat and tried again. "I am come to find the address of Lord Peter Havard. He was good enough to lend me a book of poems and I wish to return them."

The duke said nothing. He simply stared.

"Your grace?" prompted Fiona.

"I have just learned from my son that he wishes to marry you," said the duke.

"I believe so," said Fiona.

There was another long silence.

The clocks ticked, in the street outside a news-vendor blew his horn, and a log shifted in the grate with a soft sound like a sigh.

"I did not expect him to marry," said the duke at last. "It was not important to us, don't you see. My eldest son has three boys. The line is secure. No need for Havard to marry. On the other hand, if he does marry, we would expect him to know what is due to our name. Your family comes from Aberdeen, I believe."

"My father, yes," said Fiona.

The duke studied his fingernails.

"Trade?" he asked gently.

Fiona found herself growing angry. She rose to her feet. "Yes, trade, your grace," she said. "A vulgar but profitable business in jute."

"Jute?" echoed the duke. "Pray sit down, Miss Macleod. I have not finished talking to you."

"But *I* see no point in talking to *you* further," snapped Fiona. "You obviously do not consider me good enough."

"Sit down. sit down." He gave her a sudden charming smile. "And who owns these jute mills now?"

"I do," said Fiona, sitting down, but looking ruffled. "Of course, they are run by a manager, but my income comes from them."

"How much income?" asked the duke.

Fiona looked at him coldly. "Fifty thousand a year, I believe."

The duke's eyes widened a fraction. Then he smiled

137

again. "How you bristle up, Miss Macleod. But you must admit your calling here without your maid looks a trifle odd. It has come as a shock to us, this engagement. But a pleasant shock, I assure you. You must meet my wife. She will be anxious to offer you her felicitations."

"Your grace," said Fiona desperately. "I must have your son's address."

"Oh, that? St. James's Square, number sixty-five." He stood up and held out his arm and again that charming smile lit up his heavy features. "Come, Miss Macleod. You cannot possibly refuse to meet your future mother-in-law."

Fiona gave in. She allowed him to lead her up the stairs and into the long saloon at the top.

"My dear," said the duke, urging Fiona forward until she stood in front of the duchess, "Miss Macleod. Miss Macleod, my wife."

As Fiona curtsied low, the duchess glared awfully at her husband, who silently mouthed over Fiona's bent head, "Fifty thousand a year."

By the time Fiona raised her head it was to find the duchess smiling down on her. "Sit by me, child," said the duchess, patting the sofa beside her. "We must become better acquainted."

It was an hour before Fiona got away. She had to accept the escort of one of the Penshires' footmen. At the corner of Berkeley Square, she firmly dismissed the footman and said she preferred to walk alone. She knew the duke and duchess would consider such behavior eccentric in the extreme when they heard of it, but she now knew her fortune would make such eccentricities bearable.

She longed to go and see Lord Peter. Now she had his address. All she had to do was go there. But her courage had run out and instead she made her way miserably back to Holles Street.

Mr. Haddon, Amy, and Effy were seated at the dinner table. There was an air of strain about the three of them. Amy was busy hating Effy, Effy was hating Amy, and Mr. Haddon was wondering if he had done something to offend his old friends.

Disappointed in Fiona, Effy returned to the problem that had been nagging her for days. Where had Amy been when she had returned with Mr. Haddon in his carriage on the day of the duel, and why had she been wearing strange clothes?

She had accused Amy of having gone to "spoil her duel," and Amy had replied crossly that there had been no duel to spoil and had firmly lied and protested she had not gone anywhere near Chalk Farm. She said instead that Mr. Haddon had met her in Oxford Street and had taken her up on his road back and had told her that Mr. Callaghan had proved to be a coward.

Amy and Mr. Haddon had taken a long time making their way back to London. Mr. Haddon had left Amy at an inn and had gone to purchase a ready-made gown for her and a bonnet. Then they had had a pleasant meal together and an amicable drive back to London, Mr. Haddon vowing never to tell anyone of Amy's escapade.

Amy's pleasure in her day had been short-lived, for Effy had once more begun to flirt with Mr. Haddon and call him her hero.

Mr. Haddon finally broke the tense silence by asking whether Miss Macleod intended to join them for dinner.

"Let her stay in her room," snapped Amy. "I don't want to set eyes on her again."

"Why?" asked Mr. Haddon.

Effy and Amy exchanged glances. "She has announced she is to wed Lord Peter Havard," said Amy. "We do not consider it a suitable match, but it appears he has won the consent of Mr. and Mrs. Burgess."

"Splendid!" cried Mr. Haddon. "Another success, ladies."

Then he looked from Amy's angry face to Effy's downcast one. "Something has gone wrong," he said quickly. "Pray tell me what it is, my dear friends."

"It's that wretched girl," Amy blurted out. "When Captain Freddy Beaumont proposed to her, she must needs put him off by saying she was not a virgin."

"Oh, dear," murmured Mr. Haddon.

"Worse to come," went on Amy. "It seems that the captain must have told Lord Peter and Lord Peter taxed Fiona with it and the silly girl let him think it true. He ups and says he'll marry her anyway, but at a quiet wedding, here. A rushed and furtive job. No church, no bells, no mentions in the society columns."

"But all she has to do is tell him the truth!" exclaimed Mr. Haddon.

"Sounds easy," said Amy gloomily. "But the fact is Lord Peter is only human and thinks he's doing a monstrous noble thing. If she ups and tells him she was lying, he might be so exasperated, he'd call the whole thing off."

"Perhaps that might be the best thing," said Mr. Haddon. "You do not consider Lord Peter suitable. Miss Macleod is an heiress and is being courted by Aubrey, for example. She would soon find someone else."

"Fiona is in love with Lord Peter," said Effy.

"How can you tell?" snorted Amy.

"Oh, the way she looks at him," said Effy dreamily, "the way she yearns for him. I can see it in her eyes."

Mr. Haddon gave Effy a warm smile and Amy's temper snapped.

"Fustian. That chit has as much idea of love and romance as a . . . as a pig's arse!"

140

Amy saw the set lines of Mr. Haddon's face and blushed. "Sorry," she mumbled. "But it's enough to try the patience of a saint."

"I think," said Mr. Haddon slowly, "that both of you are forgetting the nature of your job. You advertised for difficult girls. Miss Macleod has been made difficult by harsh treatment by her uncle and aunt. But there is a certain sweetness and kindness about her. She has become fond of you both. Where is she now? Does she know you are furious with her? Why is she not joining us for dinner?"

"Truth to tell," said Amy, "I could not bear the sight of her. I was so disappointed we were not to have a grand wedding. I am a brute, I declare. I shall go to her room directly and bring her down."

Amy made her way up to Fiona's room. Fiona was sitting by the window, staring into space. She was still wearing her outdoor clothes. She looked so wretched that Amy ran towards her, crying, "Do not be so sad. It will all come about."

"I went to his parents' house," said Fiona in a low voice. "I got his address from them. Oh, I was all ready to go. But then, I felt so wretched. How can I tell him?"

"Effy was right," said Amy. "You *are* in love with him." She took Fiona's hands in her own. "Look, my child, I am going to urge you to do an unconventional thing. Go to him and confess the truth. No marriage can be built on a lie. He loves you, I am sure he must. I see now you would never be happy with anyone else."

Fiona shifted restlessly. "Where can I find the courage?"

"Don't try," urged Amy. "Just go. Just get up and go. Come, I shall take you outside and put you in a hack."

Fussing and pulling and pushing, Amy drove Fiona before her down the stairs. Outside, she called a passing hack. Then she seized Fiona roughly in her arms and gave her a hearty kiss on the cheek. "If I have made a mistake," muttered Amy, "don't blame me."

The hack rolled off and Amy went upstairs to join the others.

"Sitting in her room, moping," said Amy cheerfully. "But I had a talk with her and persuaded her that everything will work out."

"Is she going to tell him the truth?" asked Effy.

But Amy was already regretting her own unconventional advice. "I think she will," she said. "Why do we not play a hand of whist?"

The lamplighters were already lighting the lamps in St. James's Square when Fiona reached it. She prayed Lord Peter would be at home. Now that she was actually on his doorstep, she felt she had to go on. She had forgotten to take any money for a hack or a chair back and dreaded walking through the streets unescorted.

Lord Peter's butler looked shocked when she asked to see his master. He took her card, told her to wait, and then shut the door firmly in her face.

Fiona was furious. She felt almost naked, standing alone on that doorstep while a curious butler from next door stared at her with all the flat-eyed insolence of his betters.

She was just about to turn away when the door opened and the butler, this time flustered and obsequious, begged her to enter.

Another library to wait in, thought Fiona gloomily as the door to the book-lined room closed behind her. They always put people of uncertain status in the library.

After some time, the door opened again and Fiona

looked up hopefully. But it was only the butler again, this time bearing a tea-tray, which he set in front of her.

She sat miserably while he poured tea, wondering if Lord Peter would ever appear. She refused to take milk in her tea, having, like most of London, been put off the very idea of milk in tea by learning that the fourth Duke of Queensberry took his early-morning bath in that liquid before it was retailed.

If she had been able to get Lord Peter's address quickly, thought Fiona, then it would have been so much easier to tell him the truth. She could now feel her courage ebbing away like the light outside.

But at last the door opened and Lord Peter came in.

He stood for a moment studying Fiona. She was wearing a dress of soft blue sarsenet edged round the hem with silver cord. Over the dress was a short coat of blue satin. Her head-dress was a small blue satin cap with square corners trimmed with silver lace and tassels, and ornamented in the front with a silver spray. She had a fine rope of pearls about her neck and little pearl ear-rings.

"You should not have come here alone and unescorted," said Lord Peter, "and wearing such finery."

He crossed to the fireplace and looked down at her.

"I had to come," said Fiona.

"Yes," he agreed. "You have made me very angry."

"I am going to make you even angrier," said Fiona in a small voice.

"Now, what other horrible confession have you to make?" he demanded harshly. "Who else has been in your bed? The groom? The stable-boy?"

Fiona shrank back. Here it was, what she had dreaded, the anger, the accusations, and yet she had brought it all on herself.

"I wish to release you from the engagement," she said, mustering what dignity she could and rising to her feet.

He jerked her into his arms and looked down into her frightened eyes. "Oh, you little liar," he said softly. "I could shake you. You nearly had me believing that rubbish."

"How did you know I was lying?" asked Fiona.

"I had only to think about you. At first, because of your fire and passion and my raging jealousy, my sweet, I was inclined to believe the worst. When you called, I was taking a bath—which is why I kept you waiting so long—and realizing what a fool I had been. But you must tell me why you lied, Fiona. Obviously you did not want to accept the captain, but why not simply tell him so?"

She sighed and leaned her head against his chest. "I am so frightened of marriage," she said. "And frightened of being coerced into it. My parents were always quarrelling. Even when I went to bed at night, I could hear their voices rising and falling. They did not share the same bedchamber, but my father would visit my mother's bedchamber before retiring to his own to tell her exactly what he thought of her." Then, in a halting voice, she told him of her friendship with the servant and her subsequent humiliation, of the other proposals and how she had lied and lied to her uncle and aunt so that, in their humiliation and fury, they would not approach any suitor's parents and arrange a marriage.

"Perhaps your parents loved each other very much," he said at last. "No, do not look so surprised. Love has many peculiar faces. I had an aunt and uncle who were always quarrelling. They would make hurtful remarks to each other in public and worse remarks in private. Then my uncle died, and my aunt, to everyone's amazement, was distraught with grief and did not survive him very long. Love is not like the story-books. Oh, we shall quarrel. I shall be jealous of every man you smile on, and I hope you will be jealous every time I pay attention to some female.

144

Perhaps sometimes, to *our* children, we shall seem a most unsuited couple, but marriage is like life—exhilarating, dreadful, and often unfair. I trust we shall not ever behave so cruelly or so unnaturally as your parents towards our own children. But we shall know through thick and thin that we love each other, and that is all that matters."

"But you are a rake," whispered Fiona, "and rakes never reform."

"I think this one has," he said. "I am sure I have. But you must trust that I shall never be unfaithful to you and I must trust that you will never lie to me again. Now, I think we should go and tell your odd guardians that they may celebrate their success with a church wedding. Look at me and say that you love me and want to marry me."

He set her away from him and searched the expression in her eyes in the darkening room.

"Yes, I will marry you, and yes, I do love you," said Fiona.

"Then just one kiss and I shall take you back." But the room was warm and dark and the one kiss led to more, each subsequent kiss deeper and more lingering than the last as their bodies caught fire from each other. At last he freed his lips. "You must not see Aubrey again," he said huskily. "Promise me that."

"Anything," sighed Fiona happily, and then began to tremble as his hand slid down the front of her gown.

"No, perhaps not yet," he said, removing his hand and caressing her cheek. "But very soon . . ."

Effy threw down her cards and murmuring an excuse left the room. Amy looked after her anxiously. She hoped she was not going to visit Fiona and find that young miss gone. Sharp pangs of conscience were beginning to plague

Amy. She had sent a young girl out alone to a man's house.

Effy came back looking flushed and upset. "Fiona is not in her room," she cried, "and I cannot get a word of sense out of Harris, who keeps going on about Bertha, the chambermaid, having gone missing. Oh, Amy, what if she has left us? What did you say to her?"

"Just told her to tell the truth," mumbled Amy.

"Look at me, Amy Tribble!" cried Effy. "You're *blushing!*"

"No, I ain't!"

"Oh, yes you are. You said something to that girl in your rough, coarse way which frightened the life out of her. Tell me where she is or I shall send for the parish constable!"

Amy hung her head.

"She's at Lord Peter's."

"Did you not try to stop her, Miss Amy?" expostulated Mr. Haddon. "A young unmarried girl to visit a bachelor at his town house!"

"Oh, why am I always wrong?" shouted Amy. "Why is my life nothing but a drawful of shrunken garters?"

"Lawks!" screeched Effy. "You told her to go, Amy."

Amy bowed her head in assent.

Mr. Haddon got to his feet. "Then I suggest, ladies, we leave all recriminations until later. We must go now and rescue her from her folly."

"*Her* folly!" cried Effy, but Mr. Haddon was already on his road out of the door.

Mr. Haddon had not come in his carriage. Effy sent the footman, Henry, round to the livery stables. There was a rout being held in the house next door and it seemed an age before the rented carriage and driver could make his way through the press.

All London was coming alive for the night as their

carriage began to inch its way through the streets. It was not very far to St. James's Square, but to Amy, suffering badly as she was from a guilty conscience, the distance seemed to stretch for miles.

They received a sharp setback when Lord Peter's butler answered the door and said firmly his master was not at home.

As far as the butler was concerned, his master, for reasons best known to himself, was entertaining some high-class doxy in his library. And such goings-on to the butler spelled out "not at home" to everyone and anyone. The fact that Fiona had called at a man's home and without a maid put her firmly in the category of Fashionable Impure.

But like the good members of the ton they all were, the Tribble sisters and Mr. Haddon realized that not at home usually meant not available. Had Lord Peter already left Town, then his servant would surely have said so.

"We are here to collect Lord Peter's fiancée, Miss Fiona Macleod," he said, standing his ground.

The butler stood for a moment, remembering the name on that card.

"In that case," he said, "I will see if his lordship is available."

He ushered them into the hall and then made his way to the library.

Good servants were not supposed to knock. He rattled the doorknob loudly, scratched the door panel, and then made his way inside. Lord Peter was arranging his cravat at the glass and the lady was standing by the window.

"A gentleman and two ladies have called, my lord," said the butler. "They are come to see Miss Macleod."

"Show them in," said Lord Peter cheerfully. He turned to Fiona. "If I am not mistaken, my sweeting, your duennas have arrived, bringing Mr. Haddon with them."

Amy and Effy came hurrying in, closely followed by Mr. Haddon. Fiona turned away, anxious to compose her expression. Lord Peter had been ruthlessly kissing her "just one more time" when the butler had rattled the doorknob, and Fiona still felt shaken by her dizzying drop from the heights of passion.

Amy and Effy misunderstood her averted face.

Amy ran forward and threw her arms about Fiona and hugged her close to her flat chest. "There, there, child," said Amy. "I am a beast and a brute to have urged you into this folly. You are Amy's darling, and she shall find you a gentleman who will appreciate you."

"Miss Macleod has already found a gentleman who appreciates her," said Lord Peter, exasperated. "If you continue to interfere in my marriage plans, then I shall be very angry indeed."

"We are to be married, dear Miss Amy," said Fiona, trying to disengage herself from Amy's fierce embrace. "Really! In church, too."

"Oh," said Effy, sitting down suddenly. "I am so relieved. So very relieved." She began to cry. It was an age when gentlemen were supposed to show sensibility on all occasions, and so Mr. Haddon gallantly cried as well. Overcome with a mixture of see-sawing emotions, Fiona burst into tears, and Amy, deeply affected by the sight of Mr. Haddon's tears, began to roar and bawl.

"Dear me," said Lord Peter. "This is more like a wake than the celebration of a wedding. Champagne, Roberts," he called to his amazed butler, who was hovering nervously in the doorway.

Soon the tears were dried and they were all sipping champagne. Fiona and Lord Peter sat side by side and listened with amusement as the sisters battled over the arrangements for the wedding and whether to allow Fiona to wear a veil or not.

While the Tribble sisters argued over their glasses of champagne, their chambermaid, Bertha, was sitting in beatific state in Frank's new trap, heading rapidly out of London.

Frank had decided to adopt the disguise of commercial traveller until such time as he could find a place to settle down. His trap was one of Alford's best fifty-guinea ones, painted black, picked out in light blue, with a cane back, tilbury springs, and black and blue harness drawn by a neat little brown mare. His new sandy whiskers were partially hidden by a dashing, spotted cashmere shawl. His upper coat was a handsome blue Taglioni with a small velvet collar. A large box coat with many capes and a curricle collar was thrown over the back of the gig. His inner coat was a bright blue cutaway with gilt buttons, his waistcoat, a crimson silk and worsted with black checks and a white spot in the centre. Boots of Spanish leather and a silver mounted whip with his name inscribed on the ferrule completed his rig.

Bertha leaned against him, her eyes half closed, relishing every minute of the journey. When Frank had told her that he had come into money and added that it was Mr. Callaghan's money, Bertha thought he had only taken what rightly belonged to him. Any master refusing to pay wages deserved to be punished.

They stopped at an inn for supper and went in to the Traveller's Room, which was already full of drapers, druggists, dysalters, grocers, hop merchants, and representatives of a dozen other trades. Conversation rose and fell about their table. A hop merchant was bemoaning the blight of the last crop, a druggist was complaining that no one wanted bark anymore or isinglass for that matter, and a draper was showing samples of spring patterns. Bertha began to feel the first qualm of unease. All these gentle-men *had* jobs. How were they going to live after the stolen money and goods ran out?

"Why the long face?" asked Frank. "Here we both are, as free as the birds, and you suddenly look as if you're at a funeral."

"I was thinking," said Bertha. "What are we going to do for money, in the bye and bye, I mean."

Frank laid a finger alongside his nose and drooped his eyelid in a broad wink. "I'm going to do to others wot Mr. Callaghan did to me."

"Whatever can you mean?" cried Bertha, her eyes like saucers.

"All that equality lark," said Frank. "It touched me here." He struck his chest. "Then I learned it was all a hum. That Bond Street Beau was just working me up so's to cause trouble. But I'm going to get some books and read all that stuff by Thomas Paine and I'm going to learn speeches and I'm going to preach equality up and down the south of England."

"But how will that get you money?" cried Bertha.

"I go round with the hat and ask for donations to help the poor and suffering—the poor and suffering being me and thee."

"Ooo! You're ever so clever," said Bertha, giving his arm a squeeze.

"I know," said the ex-footman, and with a lordly wave of his hand, he summoned the waiter.

Mr. Callaghan was travelling down the dusty Dover road, on his way to France. At first, it had been a night-mare journey. Every time a carriage came alongside, Mr. Callaghan dreaded to see Mr. Haddon's furious face pok-ing out of the window. But as the miles rolled by, he began to feel secure—and sulky. The more he brooded on his misfortune, the more he became sure that the Tribble sisters had deliberately sent Frank into his employ to ruin him. They had driven him away from all the comforts of Town, the lounge in Bond Street, the drives in the Park, the clubs and routs, operas and plays. One day he would make them suffer.

He thought he had been a gullible fool to have believed Effy's story that her only money had come from what she earned. Mr. Callaghan, who gambled heavily and wasted money on showy clothes and showy horses, could not understand the budgeting of people who did not.

Somehow, some way, some time, he would hit upon a plan to ruin the Tribbles.

Chapter 10

. . . bright, and fierce, and fickle . . .
—Tennyson

THE SISTERS WERE EXALTED
with success when the news of Lord
Peter Havard's engagement burst upon the surprised
world. The world, of course, began at St. James's Square
and ended at Kensington Palace. Anyone outside that
magic sphere did not exist.

Mr. Haddon had travelled to the country to visit an old
friend, and so there was no one to curb the Tribbles' flying
spirits, or to point out to them that they were well on their
way to ruining a promising career. Fiona was wrapped up
in her own happiness and did not notice what they were
about, and Lord Peter was down in Kent.

For once Amy and Effy were in agreement over their

latest piece of madness. They had rented an open carriage, lined with blue silk and bedecked with silk roses. And they'd had a large placard made, painted in gold curly letters, and affixed to the back. On it was proclaimed, "The Misses Tribble, Chaperones Extraordinary. No Miss Is Too Difficult for Us to Hone and Refine."

Then they went driving in this equipage in the Park at the fashionable hour. The Honourable Geoffrey "Cully" Coudrey took one appalled look and headed for his club to send an express to Lord Peter. The Duchess of Penshire turned scarlet with rage and cut the Tribbles, turning her head away and pointedly ignoring their greeting, and the gossip writers from the magazines and newspapers gleefully took notes.

But the sisters were still blissfully unaware of their disgrace. They agreed that the duchess must have mistaken them for two other ladies. There were plenty of society members, mostly foppish young men, to crowd round the carriage when they stopped, twittering with delight and telling them it was a famous idea.

Fiona was rudely jerked off her pink cloud that evening to land to earth with a bump, open her eyes, and realize her chaperones were well on the way to making themselves—and her—ridiculous.

After dinner, when they were seated comfortably over the tea-tray in the drawing-room, Amy produced sheets of paper and started to draft out an advertisement. "Let me see," she said dreamily, "we shall put something like . . . um . . . 'Witness our latest success. Miss Fiona Macleod is to marry Lord Peter Havard.' Yes, and perhaps, dear Fiona, a little tribute from you."

Fiona carefully put down the sampler she had been laboriously stitching and said, "Do not be ridiculous. You must be joking."

"It pays to advertise," said Amy, unaware of Fiona's

distress. "You should have seen the faces when we drove our rig in the Park."

"What rig?" asked Fiona.

"The sweetest little chariot." Effy sighed. "We had it bedecked with flowers and a neat board on the back advertising our prowess.

"How could you?" demanded Fiona, her face flaming. "Not only have you made laughing-stocks of yourselves, but of me too."

"Nonsense!" said Amy. "Everyone was most intrigued. Mr. Cecil Delisle declared himself quite enchanted."

"Mr. Cecil Delisle is a painted and malicious gossip," said Fiona. And, made cruel by her feelings of outrage, she added, "You should have heard his remarks on your singing at the Dunsters' party. I heard him tell Lord Aubrey that if his horse could sing, he is sure it would sound and look just like you."

"You nasty little girl," roared Amy. "Go to your room. After all we have done for you . . ."

"All you have done," said Fiona stiffly, "is to do something that might stop me marrying the man I love."

She turned and walked from the room.

Effy patted Amy's hand. "Pay no attention," she said. "Bride nerves."

Amy shifted uncomfortably. "Oh, Lor, Effy, do you think . . . ?"

The door opened and the butler, Harris, came in. He handed them a letter. "Came by hand," he said. "The Duke of Penshire's footman."

"That will be all, Harris," said Amy grandly. When the butler had left, she looked at Effy's stricken face. "Don't look like that," she said. "It will be about the wedding arrangements. So kind of them to offer their town mansion."

She crackled open the heavy parchment and began to

read. Her face turned a muddy colour, and as Effy watched, Amy picked up a large quizzing-glass from the table beside her and studied the letter again.

"Don't just sit there, reading and reading," squeaked Effy. "Out with it! What does it say?"

"The duchess says," said Amy heavily, "that we are a disgrace, that we are vulgar and common. She says that she and her husband cannot bless the marriage. Lord Peter is well over age and must do as he likes, but they will no longer be a party to it."

"Ruined!" said Effy, aghast. She began to cry helplessly, saying in a choking voice between sobs that Mr. Haddon was their only hope.

"We did not do anything so very wrong," blustered Amy. "I will not apologize to Fiona, nor to the Penshires!"

But for the next week the house in Holles Street was shrouded in gloom. Fiona went for long walks and played the piano for hours and spoke only when spoken to.

Effy prayed that Mr. Haddon would come.

Come he did at last on a morning of gloomy rain. But just before his arrival, the sisters had received another blow. The Season was only a week away and the stern patronesses of Almack's Assembly Rooms in King Street had written to say they could not allow Miss Macleod vouchers. The sisters did not know that this decision had been reached before their self-advertising display. Engaged to Lord Peter Havard she might be, but Miss Macleod's own family was not distinguished enough to allow her the honour of being seen at Almack's.

Mr. Haddon surveyed the dismal scene, Effy in tears and Amy tight-faced and red-eyed.

In his usual way, he sat down patiently and listened hard to the almost incoherent explanations and excuses.

Then they both looked at him hopefully, like sinners waiting for the priest's blessing.

But he shook his head. "You have done a great deal of damage," he said, "and I do not know how you can possibly repair it. No one will want to send their daughter to you after such a public display. But that is as nothing compared to the wrong you have done Miss Macleod."

"Perhaps Lord Peter . . ." began Amy hopefully.

Mr. Haddon shook his head. "He will be furious and perhaps all too glad to settle for a quiet wedding." He held up his hand. "No, not another word. Let me think!"

Amy went to Effy and gathered her in her arms and the sisters sat side by side on the sofa, holding each other for comfort.

Mr. Haddon turned over in his mind what he knew of the Duke and Duchess of Penshire. Everyone in London society knew everyone else, like members of an exclusive club. The Penshires were acquisitive, grasping, enormously wealthy, but always on the look-out to increase the family wealth—hence their initial acceptance of Fiona. As a ducal son, there was little fear that Lord Peter would turn out to be the same. Brought up as he had been by tutors, school, and more tutors at Oxford, he had never been under any parental influence.

"I cannot promise you anything," he said at last. "But I might be able to do something."

They watched him take his leave without much hope.

They were leaning their heads together and talking in low voices when Fiona entered the room and at the same time Lord Peter Havard was announced.

He bowed to the sisters, who rose and curtsied and looked at him miserably.

"Leave us," said Fiona sternly. "I wish to speak to my fiancé in private."

Amy and Effy were too crushed to protest.

"You have changed roles, my sweet," said Lord Peter.

"Goodness, I feel I have been away for years. Come and kiss me!"

"Not yet," said Fiona. "Something disastrous has happened."

While Lord Peter held her hands in his, Fiona told him of the sisters' iniquities. She heard a stifled chuckle and looked up in amazement to find Lord Peter's eyes dancing with laughter.

"How can you laugh?" asked Fiona, pulling her hands away.

"Because it does not matter," he said. "My friend, Mr. Coudrey, wrote to me express in Kent to tell me of that affair in the Park. I set out for London immediately and by chance I met our Prince Regent on the road. He congratulated me on my marriage and I boldly told him of the Misses Tribble's advertising efforts and he laughed so hard I thought he was going to have a spasm. He had already heard of Miss Amy's singing and he says he must meet them. He is coming to our wedding and so your chaperones will have all the success they crave. But *we* do not need fashionable blessing. We have each other, and, oh, Fiona, such a sweet home in Kent."

"But your parents . . . ?"

"They will come about. Why are we wasting time? We are alone. Kiss me."

"Oh, Peter."

"And again. And again."

"We cannot leave them alone in there," bleated Effy, hanging on to Amy. Both sisters were huddled together on the landing.

"Don't see how we can do anything else," mourned Amy. "She don't want us. Nobody wants us. And Mr. Haddon is a good and kind man, but we've gone too far this time, Effy. I wonder whether there is madness in our family."

The Duke and Duchess of Penshire gracefully agreed to give audience to Mr. Haddon. They knew he was a nabob who had made a great fortune in India. But the minute they heard the reason for his call, their faces hardened.

"Havard must do as he pleases," said the duke, as usual referring to his younger son as if speaking about some unrelated member of society. "But we will not be party to the Misses Tribble's vulgarity."

"They are very great ladies," said Mr. Haddon, "who are striving to earn their keep in a genteel manner. They are well aware they have offended you and charged me to bring their apologies with this present"—he indicated a packet on his lap—"but if your minds are set against them, I shall return the present."

Two pairs of hard, acquisitive, aristocratic eyes fastened on the packet. "What is it?" asked the duke.

"I do not know," said Mr. Haddon, although he knew very well. He had brought back a collection of fine jewels from India and the one in the little packet was the prize. It was a large pigeon's-egg ruby, estimated to be one of the finest ever to come out of India. "Shall I open it? I can always wrap it again and say you refused it out of hand."

"It would be interesting to see what trifle they sent," said the duchess curiously. "The insult to our name was great." By which she meant that the present should therefore be valuable enough to cancel out that insult.

Mr. Haddon slowly unwrapped the packet, revealing a flat square box of red morocco leather. The day was dark and rainy and the oil lamps in the saloon had been lit. He clicked open the box and held it under the light of an oil lamp on a console table beside him.

Blazing with fire, red, wicked as sin, the large ruby shone with an evil light.

The duke and duchess rose as one person. Mr. Haddon rose at the same time and the three stared down at the jewel.

"Gracious," said the duchess faintly. "Why must they work when this is worth a king's ransom?"

"They have a few items," lied Mr. Haddon, "which have been in their family for a long time. They would do anything rather than part with them, but their reputation is dearer to them than any jewel."

"We accept," said the duchess breathlessly. "Pray tell Miss Amy and Miss Effy to call on me this afternoon so we can discuss arrangements for the wedding reception—to be held here, of course!"

Mr. Haddon bowed and handed her the box. Like twins, the duke and duchess sat down on the sofa together and gazed at the jewel.

"Pray do not refer to the jewel," said Mr. Haddon. "The Tribbles were afraid you might consider their great generosity a trifle vulgar."

"No, no," they chorused, still looking at the ruby. "We are vastly pleased."

Mr. Haddon bowed his way out. He could hardly wait to get back to Holles Street to tell the sisters the glad news.

Before he entered the drawing-room, he could feel the mourning atmosphere of the house had changed. When he entered, he found the reason. Lord Peter and Fiona were sitting together, looking happy and relaxed. Effy and Amy, who had finally plucked up their courage to interrupt the pair, had just heard the news of the Prince Regent's intention to attend the wedding.

In a mild voice, Mr. Haddon told them that the Duke and Duchess of Penshire had forgiven all.

When Amy and Effy's cries of rapture had died down,

Lord Peter asked curiously, "How did you manage it, Mr. Haddon?"

"Your parents were most forgiving and understanding," said Mr. Haddon. "I merely conveyed the Misses Tribble's apologies and presented them with a trifle."

"A present!" said Effy. "We must repay you. What was it?"

"A little bagatelle I happened to have at home," said Mr. Haddon. "A nonsense, I assure you."

Lord Peter looked shrewdly at the nabob. He knew his parents and knew the present must have cost Mr. Haddon dear.

Mr. Haddon returned Lord Peter's gaze with a slight look of warning in his steady grey eyes which only Fiona and Lord Peter noticed.

Amy and Effy were hugging each other in delight. Lord Peter's eyes turned to the sisters. Had Mr. Haddon's gesture been purely altruistic, or was he in love with one of the strange pair? It could be Effy with her silver hair and dainty ways and delicate skin. But there was a gallantry about Amy and a directness that might appeal to the nabob.

Mr. Haddon fell silent. He was worrying again about the future of his old friends. The wedding would be a social success, yes, but a social success for Fiona Macleod. Society would not soon forget that vulgar advertising display in the Park. Would anyone now dare to send their daughter into such a household? Mr. Haddon could only pray that somewhere in England there was some family desperate enough. It took a whole three months for his prayers even to begin to be answered.

Squire Simon Wraxall should have been a happy man. He had a handsome house, broad, prosperous acres, and one of the most beautiful daughters in the county. Delilah had recently inherited a handsome fortune from her aunt. She had everything any lady could desire—money, looks, and a comfortable home.

Except for one thing. Delilah Wraxall was twenty-three and still unwed.

The squire walked faster as if hoping to outstride his troubles. It was his late wife's fault, he thought gloomily. Whatever had possessed the wretched woman to insist on christening the girl, Delilah? Just asking for trouble.

And the trouble had been going on for some time. On her seventeenth birthday, Delilah had been a different creature, happy, gentle and kind. She had been all set to become engaged to a baronet, Sir Charles Digby. Sir Charles was a handsome young man, admittedly rather cold and over-elegant, and Delilah had obviously been in love with him. Then Sir Charles had gone away to London and, on his return, had announced he had enlisted in the army. He did not call on Delilah before his departure. She had gone about for months, silent and downcast. And then she had begun to live up to her name.

Surely there were no more hearts in the county of Kent left for her to break, thought the squire savagely. He found he had come to the outskirts of the village of Hoppelton, which boasted a good inn. He decided to go into the tap and comfort himself with a pint of brown ale.

There was a familiar gorillalike figure sitting in the bay at the window. The squire, whose eyesight was not very good, moved forward for a better look and then recognized the squat figure and heavy features of the Honourable Geoffrey Coudrey.

The squire hailed him with delight. He had been a close friend of Cully's father and had known Cully when he had been in short coats.

"What brings you here?" asked the squire when they

had settled down at the window table facing each other.

"I'm on the road back to London. I've sold my place here to Lord Peter Havard," said Cully. "He's getting married and wants to settle down."

"Thought that would never happen," said the squire. "Bit of a rake."

"Mostly gossip," said Cully. "Mind you, he's marrying a fine girl. Unusual. Background of trade and as rich as Croesus."

"Where on earth did he meet this girl?"

"There's a couple of old eccentrics called Tribble, twin sisters, bon ton, got a house in London. It seems they bring out girls damned as being difficult. Not that anyone seems to know anything difficult about Miss Macleod. Sweetest little charmer you ever saw. Still, the Tribbles got her into Peter's orbit, and with her sort of background that was quite an achievement."

"What do they mean by 'difficult'?" asked the squire, studying his glass of ale.

"Lot of gossip about that. Seems parents these days spoil the girls something dreadful. Still lash the boys to pieces, but the little misses are not expected to do anything but lisp and sew and look pretty—not like the old days," went on thirty-year-old Cully with all the sententiousness of an ancient, "where they had to know how to do everything better than their servants. Stands to reason, their minds get weak and full of fancies."

"So what do these women do?"

"Well, they run a sort of school for manners, teach 'em how to behave prettily as well as seeing they are expert at all the accomplishments—anyway that's what I gathered. They never let up, go on right to the wedding. Last time I called on little Miss Macleod—there she was, bent over her sewing which she said she hated, but that the sisters would not let her slack on it."

"Interesting," said the squire, affecting a yawn. "Where do these sisters reside? Some suburb?"

"No, smack bang in the middle of town. Holles Street, off Oxford Street."

The squire changed the subject and began to talk of crop rotation and Cully listened with all the boredom of a man who had recently renounced living in the country and everything to do with it.

Yvette, the Tribbles' French dressmaker, sat in her little room off the top landing and stitched away at Fiona's wedding gown. Another wedding gown, thought Yvette with a sigh. She knew the Tribbles would stay loyal to their servants as long as their money lasted and would not turn her off. Provided that they continued to find husbands for young ladies, Yvette could look forward to stitching more wardrobes for the Season and more wedding gowns for the successful.

But Yvette knew her work to be excellent. She knew that Fiona's gowns had excited interest and envy because generous-hearted Miss Macleod had told her so. Yvette longed to have enough money to start her own salon. Her hands lay idly on the folds of white satin as she saw in her mind's eye a neat shop with her name, "Madame Yvette"—ladies running businesses always affected a married title whether married or not—over the door, and perhaps, who knew? a royal coat of arms with "By Appointment to Her Majesty" on top of that.

Fortune had already smiled on her by finding her the job with the Tribbles. It had seemed like a miracle when Miss Amy had taken her out of that overcrowded slum in King's Cross where she lived cheek-by-jowl with other impoverished French emigrés, trying to eke out a living. Her parents had been of gentle birth, fleeing their homeland during the terror of the French Revolution as so many others had done. Her mother had died after giving birth to her in this foreign country and her father had not lived much longer.

Yvette fell to stitching again. One day, perhaps, fortune would smile on her again. In the meantime, dreams were free.

Despite the Tribbles' worries, Fiona, she who had been so terrified of marriage, felt she was being borne towards the day of her wedding on a cloud of happiness. After her wedding, she and her new husband were to travel to Paris and then Rome. Everything was already being corded up in trunks for her journey, from a portable dressing-case to "louse-proof" petticoats, which Fiona secretly meant to get rid of as soon as she could because they emitted a strong smell of creosote.

Wrapped in her own golden world, she failed to notice that Amy and Effy were becoming snappish with worry and fatigue. The wedding preparations were lavish, the Tribbles determined to salvage their reputations. But now that the sisters had achieved a suitable match for Fiona, the Burgesses appeared to think they had been given enough money to cover everything. Amy, because of her recent disgrace, had lost a great deal of her courage and felt she could not ask them for more.

By the day of the wedding, Amy and Effy finally woke up to the fact that once the wedding was over they would have barely enough to live on, let alone to keep a houseful of servants. Fretful with worry, they went on with the last-minute preparations, trying to look cheerful but dreading the vista of poverty that stretched out in front of them again.

Their worry showed in their dress. They had both told Yvette not to make them anything new. Something they already had in their wardrobes would suffice.

Although the Duke and Duchess of Penshire were supplying their home and servants, they had, it transpired, expected the Tribbles to pay for the catering, the hire of extra staff, and the decorations. The bill from Gunter, the confectioner's alone made Amy ill every time she thought of it.

Mr. and Mrs. Burgess were in residence in Holles Street, poking their noses everywhere and criticizing everything.

Amy and Effy nearly forgot all their worries when Fiona came down the stairs in her wedding gown. Knowing that unrelieved white would have made Fiona appear too colourless, Yvette had embellished the low neckline of the gown with silk vine leaves and had carried out the vine-leaf theme in delicate embroidery around the hem of the gown.

Mr. Burgess fussed forward to lead Fiona out to the carriage. Mrs. Burgess followed, then Effy and Amy and Mr. Haddon. Mr. Haddon was worrying about the cost of the wedding, but tried to comfort himself with the thought that surely the Burgesses must be paying for everything.

A clerk dressed in black coat and knee-breeches bowed in front of Amy and Effy as they walked outside and stood at the top of the steps. "The Misses Tribble?" he asked.

Amy nodded curtly and he handed her a letter with a plain seal.

She climbed into an open carriage behind the wedding carriage with Effy and Mr. Haddon.

"What's in that letter?" asked Mr. Haddon curiously.

"I don't know and I don't care," said Amy, turning her head away. "No doubt someone's dunning us for something."

Mr. Haddon held out his hand. "I will read it, Miss Amy. It might be more work for you."

"As you will," said Amy, surrendering the letter with a shrug, "but that fellow was a lawyer's clerk if ever I saw one."

Mr. Haddon opened the letter, read it, and then held it wordlessly out to Amy.

Amy took it, squinted at it, read it and then let out a whoop like a Red Indian. Effy snatched it, read it, and began to laugh with excitement. It was from Fiona's lawyers. The Misses Tribble were to submit all bills for the wedding to them and they would be paid by Miss Macleod, who gained control of her estate on the day of her marriage. Miss Macleod had further instructed her lawyer to send a draft of fifteen thousand guineas.

"Amy, sit down!" screamed Effy. "You'll overturn us!" For Amy was doing a war dance in the middle of the carriage, waving her arms and whooping with delight.

"Disgraceful," said Mrs. Burgess, turning back after staring at Amy. "Utterly disgraceful. I wish I had never sent you to them, Fiona. It must have been horrible."

"On the contrary," said Fiona, "arriving at the Tribbles was like coming out of hell. They have a gallantry and generosity of spirit far beyond your imagining."

"Well!" exclaimed Mrs. Burgess. "I was never so insulted . . ." And she was still nagging and complaining and exclaiming when they arrived at the church.

Amy and Effy and Mr. Haddon wept all through the service, and the rest of the guests, not to be outdone in sensibility, wept as well, including the Prince Regent, who was heard to say it was all too demned affecting for words. It was the most deliciously mournful wedding of the year.

"Quite like a hanging," said Lord Peter, helping his wife into the carriage after the ceremony. Fiona smiled at the watching sea of faces and tossed her wedding bouquet high in the air. Amy leaped for the sky with remarkable agility, caught the bouquet, and held it to her bosom. She took a little pink rose and shyly handed it to Mr. Haddon, then screamed as Effy stuck her hat-pin into her sister's elbow.

Mr. Haddon admonished them both and reminded them they still had their reputations to recover. After that, Amy and Effy behaved with ladylike decorum.

At long last, the speeches and dances were over. The happy couple had gone to Lord Peter's town house to spend the first night of their marriage before travelling abroad and were locked naked in each other's arms long before Amy and Effy returned wearily home, helped up the stairs to their drawing-room by a sympathetic Mr. Haddon.

"Well, that's that," sighed Amy. "Will there ever be another wedding, I wonder?"

"I should not be at all surprised," giggled Effy, and batted her eyelashes at Mr. Haddon.

"I mean will we get another job? You silly fool," said Amy.

"I am sure you will," said Mr. Haddon bracingly. But privately, he doubted very much that they would.

Down in Kent, Squire Wraxall pulled a sheet of paper in front of him and began to write, shifting a branch of candles nearer to him to provide a better light.

The quill pen began to scrape across the paper. "Dear Misses Tribble," began the squire and then scratched his wig in perplexity with the inky end of his pen.

How could he describe Delilah?

How could anyone describe Delilah?